I can honestly say right now that everyone who has read her book simply loved it. R. Clifford Hyde

A good mystery story with a heroine that's 'as plain as the nose on your face' but still keeps you reading.

Also by Lynda Hyde
Dead Dog Quilt Mystery
Fat Quarter Mystery

In A Mother's Heart

By Lynda Hyde

Randy's House Publishing
3807 Lord Rd
Crosby, Texas 77532

IN A MOTHER'S HEART

published by arrangement with the author
PRINTING HISTORY

For information, address:
Randy's House Publishing
3807 Lord Rd
Crosby, Texas 77532

ISBN: 978-0-578-00127-2

PRINTED IN THE UNITED STATES OF AMERICA

Cover photo and design by Randy and Lynda Hyde @2008

Dedicated to my kids and grandkids and my husband

CHAPTER 1

Well, we're finally off for a weekend away from family, telephones and Ronnie's job. But I didn't know I was getting more than I bargained for from this trip. Let me back up some here, to explain a little. My name is Suzy Lighter, short for Suzannah, retired from a large corporation which I had learned to hate after 20 years, way too much politics, but it paid the bills and added to our family income, mother of two and grandmother of four, and part time private eye. And busier now than I ever was when I worked full time. This trip to Dallas was supposed to be some down time for my husband Ronnie and me, but turned out to be just the opposite. I wanted to see the Dallas quilt show. By the way, I like to quilt in my spare time, like I have any of that but it sounds great. I always wanted to do some quilting but I was always working, but mostly for my own family so they would have something to remember me for except being a good cook, and all the whippings they say I use to hand out. So a bunch of us old hens are gabbing it up while Ronnie and some of the other dutiful and bored husbands are hanging out together when one of the ladies there, Lillian Chambers, approached me.

Lillian said, "Suzy, tell me about your private investigating work and are you any good at it and where are you from?" Boy, this lady is going to be a hard one to deal with, but I think I am going to like her.

"I am from Houston", I said, "'but as far as how good I am, you will have to be the judge of that."

Well one thing led to another and it turns out she was from Houston, Texas on the east side and we are from the Northeast side about twenty five miles out. She goes on to tell me her son Robert had disappeared about a year ago and had not been heard from since. I have learned to watch and listen how a person tells a story of personal tragedy, to see if they are really sincere. She went on to explain that he was all she had left in the world since her husband had passed away with cancer 10 years ago. Lillian said she had turned him in as missing, but he was 17 and listed as a runaway, and she was sure this was not the case, because he would never do this of his own free will, but with no proof except for knowing it in her heart, well being a mother myself, how could I argue with that. She seemed so honest and sad at the same time, and I am sure if anything happened to one of my family it would really weigh heavy on my mind as it seems to have on hers. We went over to the big dining area at the center where they were having the show and sat and talked for a long while. I wanted to get to know her a little better before I even considered taking on her case. As most mothers would say, she went on to tell me that Robert would not have just left without a word, he was too good a kid for that. But we don't really know what our kids do when we are not around, so I took that statement in with a grain of salt as they say. She went on to give me as much information about Robert and what he was interested in as for as his likes and dislikes, hobbies, friends, places he liked to hang out and so on. But when a person is missing this long you have to be very optimistic and open to all areas of thinking of what could have happened to him, as a run-away or worse, but we will cross that bridge when and if we come to it. So I accepted the case and told her I would start checking with the police and see what I could come up with.

Tears started falling down her face and she said,

"Well that's more than I have been able to get any one else to do."

As we walked back to our booth Lillian seemed a little calmer and I did not want to take another missing persons case, because most of the time they had a tragic ending, but I did not want to even think of this case in that way, and this lady really seemed like her world was shattered, by just the not knowing. Lillian asked me what my fee was and we agreed to hold off on that until we both got home which is very unusual for me to do this, but I really felt I could trust her. I did tell her what my normal charge was and she agreed to it as very reasonable.

Well the rest of the weekend was wonderful and well worth the trip, and there were so many beautiful quilts entered which, none of mine were that good yet, but maybe someday. Now Dallas is such a pretty place and lots to see and do but there was too little time to enjoy it all, but was great fun just the same. It seems that the people are still trying to live down the presidential assassination from nearly fifty years ago and made a heck of a land mark out of the book depository building where President Kennedy was shot from and is a very nice museum slash shrine for him and his family but if you lived through that time of history in the making, it seems so sad in a way, like you were actually there, and I guess for the people from Texas like us, that's the way it will always be. I remember the morning after the assassination my dad had a stroke and we had followed behind the ambulance to the hospital, and they were already selling life sized paintings of him on the street outside of the hospital. I was only seventeen at the time, but I remember it like it was yesterday. I guess a piece of history like this was, will be engraved in our minds for the rest of our lives.

So after the weekend was over I did some checking with the help of my brother in-law Arnie who is with the Houston Police Dept, but a year gone by leaves a cold trail to follow. The police did make out a missing persons report but finally backed off, and the case is still listed as unsolved at this point. I know it happens all the time, but I just do not accept that answer, unsolved. It implies that you have lost interest and hope in that person ever being found or not, and I am sure that is not true, because the police department does not usually work in that manner, each case is taken on an individual basis and does not work on the idea that one person is more important than another. But on the other hand, their job is to solve as many cases as possible. But to me that sounds so impersonal, so I started checking the computer for missing persons around about the time Robert disappeared and came up with the name of a boy that Lillian recognized as a boy that Robert used to hang out with, by the name of Jesse Daniel and this put a new light on things, with two boys missing now with no explanation, and could possibly be connected. Jesse lived with an old uncle, Mort Gunther, that wasn't concerned if he was there or not, and basically just accepted the idea that he wasn't around any longer, less trouble for him. If Jesse came up missing, Lillian wanted to know why she never heard about Jesse's disappearance and why the two cases were never linked together, a lot of unanswered questions, and Lillian wanted answers, so it was time for me to earn my fee and give them to her.

CHAPTER 2

All this started July 1st, 2006 when I was asked by Lillian to check into Roberts disappearance, which made it around June or July of 2005 when Robert came up missing, and that time of year in Texas near the Bay is like Ronnie always says it's hotter than nine kinds of hell and that's putting it mildly. The temps here can easily tip the thermometer at 100 to 106, depending on whether we have had much rain or not, which June is our rainy month. Only thing this weather is good for is to lay out on Galveston beach and soak up the sun between rains. Driving down the seawall is an eye opener, people skating on the walks and riding bicycles. Walking the beach has always been a favorite summer pastime of mine even if I don't get to do it very often. After all Galveston has so much to offer if you are interested in just hanging out on the Strand and going through all the shops and worlds of great restaurants. Everyone seems so laid back and relaxed, something we don't ordinarily let ourselves do enough of. Seems every time we have out of town company, that's the first place everyone wants to go to. And naturally I'm delighted to take them there. It's very calming and relaxing, and Lord knows we don't get enough of that in our busy lives.

I started checking out the people Robert and Jesse had dealings with and came up with a long list of names. First came the neighbors around Lillian's house, I started with the girl Robert had been dating since junior high school, Sabrina Lane, but it was all over her head and like talking to a marshmallow that had already been roasted. I don't know if it was all an act or there really are people that dumb in this world, let's hope not. The blonde hair really fit with her. "Sabrina," I asked, "were you and Robert intimate?" and she said they were not but always used birth control on their dates. And I said, "You're not understanding the question." but Sabrina had a lost look on her face so I didn't press it any further. "Are your folks home?" I asked, and Sabrina said I could talk to her mom, for a few minutes. "Mrs. Lane", I said,"I wanted to talk to you about Robert Chambers, your daughter's boyfriend and neighbor."

"Well", she said, "you are talking to the wrong person if you want to hear something good about him. Robert just took it for granted that Sabrina was always going to be around for him, just whenever he decided to come around, you know, first love and all that, and she would if I had let her, but she was not going to be treated that way if I had anything to do with it."

But I do feel sorry for Lillian, she said she is such a good person, and a loving dedicated mother, but some times your kids can just break your heart. "I can surely see that from a mother's point of view", I told her. I was kind of doing a mental scan of the back of the house and the pool, while we were talking, it was a very large kidney-shaped one with a large deck going around it and a very large porch going up to the house. She said she did not have much more to add, but she gave me the name of another girl that lived next door, Regina Carson, that was a little more interesting, but very withdrawn.

Regina's father Ernie Carson was very reluctant to have me talk to her, but finally caved in, enough for me to ask a few questions, which was a waste of time. Regina said, "I was friendly enough with Robert at school but didn't know him very well. He was a bit of a loner and stayed to himself mostly." Go figure, when Robert just lived a few doors down, but there was several acres between them. Regina's father Ernie stayed very close at hand while I was questioning her, which seemed to make Regina very uncomfortable not to mention how it made me feel. They seemed to have a nice home, well decorated and cold feeling. I would love to check out the back part of outside, but I will save that for another day. So Regina accompanied me to the door with her dad right behind her, and I said I would most likely return with more questions, and Ernie just kind of looked at me with a cold stare, a not so friendly cuss.

Now Jeffery Costner, the next neighbor on my list, was a little more agreeable and anxious to help if he could, but said he didn't remember Robert at all, only from school, another dead end. Kids have short memories conveniently sometimes, which I am very aware of in dealing with my own kids and grand kids, sometimes I wonder how they get back and forth from home by themselves without a compass. Here I was on the northeast side of Houston and I lived about 30 minutes from here and ready for my easy chair and Diet Coke and was beginning to feel the effects of my day, plus the heat, a humid 97 degrees was about to do me in.

CHAPTER 3

I went back home and checked messages and had four of them, one my trusty neighbor Mandy who wanted us to play Scrabble tonight which I could just already hear Ronnie screaming. He loves the game and loves Mandy to death, by the way she's 85 and a kicker, and he always has a good time but just the idea of going anywhere after commuting to the city and back during the week is unheard of. Next message is from my no. 2 grandson Jonathon, wanting to know if I'm cooking tonight, wants to come over and eat, which a seventeen year old has a bottomless pit for a stomach, and this is the grandson who socked me in the eye when he was 18 months old and I went to work with a black eye for a few days and had to explain that one and never heard the end of it until it had gotten well, that should have been a warning of what was in store for all of us when he grew up . His mom asked him why he hit grams and he said, “She was messing with me.” Guess I still hold a grudge after all these years. Gotta love em, huh?

His mom Annie, my daughter, decided she just couldn't stay in her marriage any longer after twenty years. The two boys really took it hard, but Jonathon had it the worse because he was the youngest and Dirk was a senior. So I try to stay as close to the kids as I can without pissing her off, but it still doesn't always work that way, seems that anything I say these days sends her straight up into orbit. Oh well, by the way, Jonathon lives with his dad, his choice of course. Next message was from Ronnie saying he was leaving Houston now, and did we need anything from the grocery store. If I say yes he gets all ruffled around the edges and if I say no he feels unneeded. What's one to do? Last message is from my son Ronnie Jr. wanting me to pickup no. 3 grandson Brent from school tomorrow. What am I, a taxi service? Well, he knows I'll do it, and only too glad, I'm surprised he didn't have Brent call me, he knows I can't turn the grand kids down for anything. I'm a sucker when it comes to them. Not spoiled, are they? No. 1 grandson Dirk is away at college and living it up. Hope he gets an education in the process somehow. And last but not least by all means miss drama queen Rennie is 12 going on 18 and keeps her dad, my son, on his toes checking her cell phone for boys calling, and watching everything she puts on to make sure it is appropriate for a twelve year old, he doesn't cut her any slack at all and I even get into trouble sometimes when I take her shopping. We always have to get Dad's seal of approval. He really has his hands full, what goes around comes around, he dealt me nothing but misery when he was growing up. There is some justice in this old world after all. Everyone tells me I should separate myself from my family, because I always want them around me and talk to them almost daily, but I just smile and tell them that if I wasn't supposed to do this then I would not have been blessed with them, and to mind their own business. I see people that live so far away from their kids and grandkids and wonder how I would deal with that, but I hope I'll never find out. I guess you do whatever you have to make the best of things and live one day at a time but I still need family to be near, but it is a real fine line between caring, and just plain butting in, which I know I get pretty close sometimes so I have to back away and give them some room to breathe and we women are just naturally nosy. I have gotten more into my business now and this keeps me from putting my foot in my mouth quite so often.

Ronnie and I try to travel some and this keeps me busy also, but it seems that every time we get out of town, we are swamped with calls from family wanting to know when we will be home, so I guess they don't think I am too much of a busy body after all.

CHAPTER 4

Today it's about 96 outside and my car, a beat-up old Chevy Cavalier that's hit too many pot holes around Houston, and it seems that the air conditioner is having trouble keeping up so I reached down to kick it up a notch and looked up just in time to see an old 70's sky blue pickup following me. I turned and he turned right behind me, so it wasn't my imagination. I pulled into a Fina station on old Hwy. 90 and the old truck went right past me. I didn't get a look at the driver but got the feeling maybe he had been following me a while, probably since I left home, so it's a safe bet that he knows exactly where I live, not a good feeling. We live on two acres with no houses around for a half a mile. I think I'll stop and call Mandy and have her go by the house and check on things and if there is anyone messing around there to call the police. I think if I was a prowler I would rather deal with the police than Mandy, if they make her mad enough she will run them over with the car or take off after them with her shotgun. Mandy is as good as any watch dog. She is a widow lady that never stops being a friend to the ones she cares about and we have been friends for years and I really enjoy having her around, but sometimes she tells me what she thinks and it's not always what I want to here, but Ronnie tells me to just keep it to myself because he thinks she is an angel on wheels, she always blows the horn when she passes by, to let you know she is in the neighborhood.

I'm going to visit another neighbor today, around Lillian's area out R.E. Kellam Drive, George Morrison, he lives down R.E. Kellam off old hwy 90 to Barnett road to Hummingbird lane, and then to Jasmine street, boy a person could get lost on all these little side streets if their not careful but it seems to be very quiet out here. Everything is not always as it seems.

George did not answer the door, so I will have to come another time but will leave him my card. With no car in the driveway I figured he was out, which gave me the excuse to check out the house for a blue pickup, ah my suspicious mind. I then called my brother-in-law Arnie to tell him about my encounter with the blue truck, just so someone knows what is going on. Arnie is married to my sister Ladonna, I'm glad someone can stand her moods and habits. He deserves a medal for that. I told Arnie about the two murder cases and he said they did not connect the two because legally Jesse lived with his father in another city, but the uncle was listed also as temporary guardian, after the father got in some trouble with the law. Supposedly he was clean now. Arnie said to be very careful and keep him posted on what I came up with. Well with that warning I decided to call my old pal Oscar Davenport, an ex cop friend. Oscar is my sometimes protector and extra snoop, the big joke with Oscar is after a bar brawl he left his job due to a personal injury that left only one family jewel, only it is not such a big joke to Oscar. He had quite a long recovery. But he says it didn't cramp his style in the least. I wanted Oscar to do some leg work for me on the other missing boy, Jesse Daniel, over in nearby Jackson where Jesse's dad Leon was last known to be living. There were questions on his whereabouts when he went missing, and if he and Robert had been in touch at that time. It seemed I had run in to a dead end until Lillian called me and said she had found a letter from someone that signed it with only G. So I hopped in my old clunker and went to Lillian's. Now I'm not one of these people who forget to eat, that's the one thing I don't have a problem remembering so I stopped at my favorite sandwich shop and got a sandwich and chips, which Ronnie laughs at me because I think you can't have a sandwich without chips and drink. It's just not normal.

By the time I got to Lillian's she was in from work, but was upset about something. The letter was about a relationship that the girls family was not happy with, so this was a possible motive for Robert's disappearance, but very little to go on.

CHAPTER 5

I asked Lillian if I could take the letter with me and she agreed after a moment of hesitation. And it was apparent that she didn't really want to part with it. Then I called Oscar to see if he had talked to Jesse's dad Leon, but he had not located him as of yet. He said he really wanted to talk to him and get an idea about what kind of kid he was, hot headed or mild, and meek, caring, responsible or not, so he was to meet me at Harry's diner on Marina Ave. in the town where I live, to discuss it. Now Cranston is not a very big town because everyone knows everyone and their business, which can get a little sticky sometimes. But if you need to know anything about anyone or anything just ask Mandy, she keeps up with it all, but in a loving and caring way. Everyone seems to know her or at least of her and every time we go out we always run into someone familiar to her. But then she has lived here most of her life.

Oscar and I discussed what I had already found on the two missing boys and decided we had to take more action by checking with some of his teachers at Humphrey High school where Robert went. So Oscar and I finished our coffee and got the tall lanky waitress with a name tag that said Judy on it to bring our ticket and bid her a good day. After I finished talking to one of Robert's teachers, she pointed out one of his classmates that she said probably knew him better than most, by the name of Rich Southerland. Now Rich was a clean enough cut kid if you liked a thug with sticky fingers. First impressions are usually the best. Rich said he had talked to Robert the day he disappeared, but did not remember a lot about their conversation that day, yeah, I guess a year is a long time for a 17 yr old to keep anything in his memory besides girls and his last meal. But Rich said he would let me know if he remembered something. I kind of wanted to walk around the school parking lot a bit to see what kind of cars were there or maybe a blue truck, especially, but one of the campus monitors stopped me to see what I was doing hanging around there for, and I told her that I was investigating the disappearance of Robert Chambers. Miss monitor said she remembered Robert and that his coming up missing was a great tragedy for all, that Robert seemed to be very promising in high school and seemed to have a good future ahead of him, and talked of going into law enforcement, but was a little high strung for his own good. I told her thank you for the help and was on my merry way once again. But in the back of my mind I was still wondering who G. was and if she had something to do with Robert's disappearance, but the day was still young and I needed to stop by the market and pick up a few things for dinner.

CHAPTER 6

We woke up to another hot, humid and drizzly 90 degrees, good ole July Texas weather, gotta love it or leave it, no big choice there. I had to have 2 to 3 cups of coffee and about an hour to wake up before I get started. Ronnie always has my coffee ready when I get up, although he doesn't drink it himself, and he leaves for work at about 6 A.M. I'm lazy and usually sleep in until 7 or so, then go for my one mile walk at the track around the park then come back home and do the shower thing. I sat at the kitchen table to have my coffee and checked through what information I had, which was not a lot.

My sister Ladonna and my brother-in-law Arnie came over last night and Arnie and I were talking about how the police work a missing person's case, especially if it is a child under 18. If a person really feels that somebody didn't show up when they were supposed to and if they don't feel that things are right, that something might have happened to this person they should file a report. Most people believe a person has to be missing for at least 24 hours, before police will take any action, but that is not true. An officer is assigned to the case and a file is opened on this person which gets circulated among officers on street patrol, but in Robert's case someone made the decision that he was a possible runaway but then later was handled as a missing person. So there was a bit of a time lapse there, that had to be figured in. Each city and state are set up differently, but this was the way it was supposed to be in Roberts case. This is so heartbreaking for Lillian, his mom, because she feels she did everything she was supposed to, but her son is still out there somewhere, and not knowing if he is dead or alive is a mothers worst fear. I re-read the letter Lillian gave me several more times thinking something would reach out and grab me that I didn't see before, but no go, so I tucked it with my little .38 snub nose revolver, that Ronnie gave me for protection in my purse and was on my way. I went to the court house to check up on some of the properties out in the neighborhood where Lillian lives, not really sure what I was looking for but it can't hurt to check it out. The lady at the records department was very helpful and gave me hints on how to find the right information and understand what I was looking at, and gave me records from the last three years. Some of the tax information on record gave me areas that had improvements in the last three years, and how property taxes are increased, the legislature determines how and in what form goes on to provide tax increases from increased property value. And how some property values are rated, such as improvements to property or adding new structures or any kind of construction to your property are maintenance, that adds value to your home and property which in plain English means you will pay more taxes. So if you want a room added to your home, you put in a pool or a new fence it will cost you twice, that is the reason you have to have permits to add anything to your property so the government can keep up with it so they can charge you more. Who ever said it was a free country? I had pretty well gotten what I came for, whatever that turns out to be, so I thanked the lady there for being so helpful and looked around to see how the courthouse was filling up with more people and was glad I was finished.

Then I got outside and was not too happy to see I had a flat on my old car, so I called the auto club for help and I had to wait for an hour for someone to come and fix it, but it gave me a little time to think things over. When I got in my car I noticed the old blue pickup in my rear-view mirror that had followed me to town, but I was getting a little tired of this. Now in Texas we have license plates on the front and the rear of the vehicle but they were not getting close enough for me to get a good look at the number, but someone was really interested in where I was going and what I was doing, so I decided to slow down and see if I could get a good look at them, but, just as I did they whipped around me and went on before I saw who or what it was. Well, I thought this is very interesting, someone doesn't want me to find out something and this is making me very nervous and more suspicious of what was really going on here.

CHAPTER 7

By afternoon I was not sure which way to turn so I called my neighbor Mandy to see what was up with her, and she wanted me to have lunch and take in a movie to clear my head which worked beautifully. She is such a joy to have around, and she can pick up any kind of mood you may be experiencing, even a confused one, which is what I'm in most of the time these days.

So after a very relaxing and calming afternoon, I called Oscar and asked him to go with me to make a second visit to the home of George Morrison, one of Lillian's neighbors who lived there with his wife and daughter. After a few minutes I guess it was the daughter Joanie who answered. She looked to be about 12 or 13 and just big enough to start giving mom and dad a long road to follow down, pre-teen, just that age for telephones, boys and lots of giggles, and I remembered my own daughter Annie, and the misery she gave me at that age, made me want to run away and live somewhere else. But Joanie called her mom into the room and left us there, to visit without her, and you know how boring parents are, and don't know as much as you do according to them. Joanie didn't give us a lot on Robert, but said he was nice enough and like everyone else I talked to thought that it was a tragedy he just seemed to go away off of the face of the earth without a trace. Mom's name was Joan, guess that's confusing with her name-sake Joanie. She went on to say that she and Lillian were not too close but had coffee together sometime and would see Robert every once in awhile, and also said, that Robert and Sabrina would drive by in

Lillian's car, but not often. She did tell us something that Lillian had failed to mention, that Robert was very good with computers and was always on the computer, so that could lead to something else to check out, we could look into some of his files and see who he is talking to and if there is more than meets the eye with it.

Oscar asked if he could have a glass of water and Joan went to get it and asked if we wanted coffee or something, I said no and Oscar said coffee, and a glass of water would be nice, leave it to a guy to want as much as he could get, but I got the feeling Oscar wanted more than water and coffee. When Joan left the room Oscar did a once over on some bills and other mail on Joan's desk, which I really didn't think of, but Oscar said Joan was too cooperative and didn't seem to be telling everything, but I have learned to let him go with his suspicions rather than argue, because he was most always right or close to right and this time was no exception. There was a letter from Drake's concrete company, telling him that the information he had requested would be sent to him in a week or ten days, that the records on the delivery had been temporarily misplaced, now what was all this about? But Oscar had to put the letter back on the desk before he was caught snooping around in there and just in time because Joan returned with our drinks, right at that moment. Boy, was that a close one, but that does not bother Oscar in the least, which is the reason I wanted him to come along. He usually picks up on the things that go right over my head and then sometimes the tables are turned, and every once in a while we both strike out, but not often, that's the reason we work so well together. Oscar is pretty well a hard ass, and doesn't get on well with most people but has never given me a minutes trouble and Ronnie likes him a lot, even if they are as different as daylight and dark, go figure. Ronnie says you have to understand him before you get along with him, he is not always as he seems, which I have found is the truth. His wife left him because she couldn't stand him being a cop but he seems a lot happier not to have her any more, and dates once in a while and says he likes to be alone most of the time, which I don't believe that for a second. He is one of those guys that wants someone around when he wants them and otherwise leave him alone. That sounds familiar, I have a divorced son the same way, so he will probably stay single a long while, so much for my perfect family. Well, back to our visit with Joan Morrison, she said her husband George would not be home from work until after six and that we could catch him then. So I asked her how long they had lived here and she said about 9 years and that they had moved down from Philadelphia when Joannie was 3, almost 4. Well I hit that one on the head, do I know kids or what, and that George was transferred down here by his company, that they didn't have too many friends here except a few of the neighbors and some of Georges co-workers but didn't mingle much except on special occasions. The rest of the interview was just small talk and so we thanked Joan for her hospitality and I told her I would be back later to talk with her husband George. Joan showed us out and I happened to look back and for an instant I saw someone look out the mini blinds, guess she wanted to make sure we were actually leaving. So Oscar and I kind of went over what we had learned from Joan and I dropped him off at his place and went on home and my phone was ringing as I went in, which was Mandy asking me to come over and help her pen up a dog that had been at my house the day before so the animal control could pick it up. I thought they had picked it up from my house but it had made its way over to hers instead. The guy was very hesitant to take the dog, it was kind of pretty and looked like someone's pet but neither of us wanted a dog. Well, so much for one dog. Gone. We live out in the country so when someone doesn't want an animal they just drop it off near one of us, I finally figured this out and quit feeding all the strays. Once we had a calico cat left here and my grandsons, Jonathon and Brent took it off with them which was Jonathon's bright idea and before they got a quarter of a mile from the house Jonathon called back to say the cat went crazy and was bouncing off the truck cab so they opened the door and it took off into the woods. Needless to say we never saw the cat again.

That evening I went back over to George's house to have a talk with him and he was not as friendly or cooperative as his wife Joan was, but I did get to ask him a few questions about the neighbors and he said that the only ones he knew was what his wife had told him, that he was not home much. But Robert did speed down the road a lot in Lillian's car, and that it was a wonder that no one was hurt. But he did say that it was kind of sad for Lillian that the boy just disappeared and no one could seem to figure out why, that no parent should have to go through that, which seemed very caring for a man to say but he seemed to be getting very agitated with me for asking so many questions so I decided to wait until another day and return maybe at a better time and earlier, because it was getting late and Ronnie would be expecting me and dinner.

The next morning we woke to another hot and steamy day but with maybe a promise of a little rain to either make it more humid or just a little cooler. I got dressed and had my coffee while I read some of what George Morrison had told me, not so much of what he said but the way he said it, almost feeling sorry for Lillian, and like Robert was gone for good. What did he know that we didn't. How did he come to this conclusion, that he made sound so final? So I guess I needed to look into this a little more.

CHAPTER 8

The next thing on my list was to go back and talk to Lillian and see why she didn't tell me about Robert's computer and just how much he was into them because there could be some very valuable evidence there, or something else she was hiding. Lillian had not left for work yet, so she had a few minutes to talk, and the first thing I asked her was what else was Robert interested in beside computers, and that anything she knew could be very helpful to the case - his likes and dislikes.

Lillian said, "Suzy, I didn't want to be snooping around Robert's things even though he's not here because I always tried to respect his privacy, but if you think it will help you can take a look, I just still have hopes that he will come home".

"Well, Lillian, did Robert have any hobbies or any sports that he was interested in?" I think I had asked this before when we first met, but never really got a straight answer.

"No, not really, none that he took part in, just liked to watch football and went to some of the school games, but mostly with friends." I wanted to look in his computer, but also I want a friend of mine to take a look at it I told her, and she said I had her permission to either take it or that we could come back tonight when she got off of work, so I chose to come back later. I would like to look around the room even it has been a year since Robert was here, but there still may be something everyone has missed, just maybe a small clue of any kind. There was a picture on the night stand that caught my eye, and I asked Lillian where this was taken and she said in the back yard over at one of the neighbors, but she wasn't sure which one. So I didn't push it at this time. There was a large swimming pool with four kids standing around it and looked like they hadn't a care in the world but having fun. Lillian was in a hurry to head on out for work so I said I would be back later to check the computer and left for my next appointment, which was to the police station to see if Arnie was in yet and chat with a couple of guys I knew. Arnie's lieutenant and the police were very busy with a lot of people coming and going. If you have ever been in a local station you know it's like a zoo, especially a large police station like this one. The guy inside the first cubicle was being questioned and was yelling at the top of his lungs and the officer looked about ready to deck him one, and I heard the officer ask him if he wanted to keep all his teeth and the guy said just try and then all hell broke out. So I moved to the next one and there was a lady, but probably not actually a lady if you know what I mean, who was dressed like a street walker and not a high class one. I finally found Arnie and was amazed to see he wasn't busy at the moment except for paper work. Arnie looked up and asked me, what are you doing down here in the pits, toots, which is a pet name he uses for most women, and about that time before I had a chance to answer a fellow officer stuck his head in and needed some information on one of the kids that was missing, and it turned out to be Robert Chambers. What are the odds of that? So Arnie included me in the conversation, and told the guy that I was investigating Robert's disappearance. I asked the guy if they had found any news on the case. He kind of wanted me to share my information with them, and they would share theirs with me, kind of you scratch my back and I'll scratch yours. The only problem with this is I had more to give them than they did. But you never know what might develop so I sat a while and talked to Arnie about who did the actual checking with neighbors from his office.

Arnie said, "Come on and I'll introduce you to him, but it is such a cold case at this point, don't expect too much."

I said ok and we went down the hall a bit and stopped at a little office that had a plant on a stand and two family pictures on the desk. I guess it was family and a picture on the wall, other than this there was just a short and pudgy man, Al, about 58 or 60 and about ready for retirement if I was going to guess and those types aren't really too gung ho about helping, just mostly counting the days until retirement. Me and my first impressions, how bad of me, now I sound like Jonathon when I told him he could not have a chocolate bunny for Easter, that it made him too hyper and he said I'm not hyper I'm just bad, Grams. But like Al I'm too old to change now.

After I told Al what I was here for and we exchanged introductions I asked, "Al, who all did you question about the disappearance of Robert and did you draw any conclusions or suspicions about any one of them?"

Al said he didn't remember all the details of the conversations but that the Carsons next door were a little nervous and were ready for him to leave, but I'm not surprised with his attitude. He said Lillian was really a worried and caring mother, he did remember that, well there may be hope for him yet. Al said that the Morrison's just remembered what a cocky kid he was and that he was a crazy and wild driver. He drove way too fast in the neighborhood and they were afraid for their daughter getting near the road while he was driving. Now Sabrina, there's a mysterious one and seems calm and meek unless you ruffle her feathers a bit, which I did and she would probably get angry easily as she appeared to be somewhat jealous of Robert and I thought she could have gotten outraged with him and possibly get even, in a very dangerous way but I could not come up with any evidence to that effect, and that is the name of the game here. I followed her to a few places and watched her a few days, but nothing turned up. And that's about all there was to my short investigation, Mrs. Lighter, I'm probably not much help to you, but there just wasn't much to go on. I thanked Al and made my way back to Arnie's office cubicle and had a cup of coffee and realized I was getting hungry, so I took Arnie to Burger King around the corner and ordered myself a Whopper and chocolate shake. I never said I was trying to be a skinny person. Arnie ordered a Whopper and Diet Coke, guess you cut calories where you can, but just the same Ladonna would have a fit if she knew he was not eating healthy, oh, I forgot to mention that my sister was a health nut. I went after lunch and dropped Arnie off back at the station and decided to go and pay miss Sabrina another visit and then go back over to Lillian's to check out the computer but first I had to call Oscar to meet me there so he could snoop a little, he is much better at it than I am and more into electronics.

CHAPTER 9

When Sabrina got home from school I was waiting on her with her mom. She looked a little surprised and confused at my being there. Now Sabrina was not as lacking of intelligence as she tried to make me believe the first time I talked with her but she was still trying to act as the mistreated girlfriend here as her mom had described and when I asked her if Robert had been seeing anyone else while he was with her, and she became furious and tried to stomp out of the room, but I stepped in front of her and that is when her true colors came out. I could almost see her eyes steaming, this child was too young to have a temper like this, and I thought Jonathon could turn on a dime, but she had him beat. I asked Sabrina if she would please sit down and just answer my questions and her mom looked her way and nodded her head giving permission for her to cooperate. Sabrina cooled down a bit and seemed to listen to mom, well that was a plus. Mrs. Lane asked if I would like to have some coffee or something stronger and I said coffee, she brought coffee and a coke for her daughter and then settled back in to listen. I told Sabrina I had to ask things she was not going to like, but it was the only way I was going to get any answers about Robert. She seemed angrier with him than finding him. But after all she was just a kid too. Who knows what goes on in their minds? Sabrina said she and Robert had been very close, and then something changed in him, and he didn't come around as often, mostly for what was in it for him as in sex. So she did suspect there was another girl involved but had never caught him. When they were at a ball game he would wander away for a while but she put up with it, and there were usually other friends she could talk to until he made his way back. He would never tell her what he was doing or where he was, he just brushed it off.

"How long are we talking about here Sabrina?"

"Oh, maybe fifteen to twenty minutes, but could have been longer", she said "I would start hanging out with other friends and lose track of time, but we would usually end up in a fight and he would take me home."

"Did you ever go to his house or he come here very often?" I asked.

"Just to swim once in a while, but not often, he always had other things to do or run errands for his mom; he was really close to her."

"Did you know Jesse Daniel?" I asked.

"Yes, Jesse lived here somewhere with his uncle and went to school with us for a while, but moved with his dad, I didn't know him real well, but Robert liked him and I know they ran around together a lot. I got the feeling he would lead Robert astray real easy if he had the chance, because he seemed to have some strange power over him that I never could figure out. Robert was easily swayed to do what someone else wanted him to do." Sabrina said and I asked her what she meant but she said she couldn't quite put her finger on what it was about him and Jesse but that he was just so different when he was around Jesse, like he was trying to be a tough guy or trying to prove something. He didn't act that way around our friends that we hung around with so it was all an act for some reason, so if Robert is in trouble you can bet Jesse is right along with him.

"I saw a picture in Robert's room of you and him and Regina and someone else. Where was this taken" I asked, "and who was the other boy, was this Jesse?"

Sabrina looked a little startled at the question but said the picture was taken in Regina's backyard, and why did I want to know and she sounded a little hostile again, like she was about to blow a fuse again with me, but soon backed off. But she couldn't remember who the other boy was and that if she saw the photo she would probably be able to tell who it was. Now my suspicious mind is working overtime. Why doesn't she just tell me who it was posing with them? But probably nothing. My son Ronnie Jr says I do not trust anyone and I guess he is partly right especially when there is reason for it. But this man that can't trust women since his divorce also says I just want friends around when I want them, but I like to think this is not true that I'm not this selfish. Sabrina looked like she was getting a little restless with all the questions so I told her I might want to talk to her later and Mom said it would be fine, to just call first to see if they were here. So I thanked the mom for the coffee and went to Lillian's a couple of doors down to meet Oscar.

Oscar was already there and striking up a conversation with Lillian, which Oscar seemed like he wanted to hit on her but I was trying to discourage him for now, but Lillian was a fairly attractive woman, not too far from his age, medium short hair and coal black, so it might be a good match for them, but first we had to take care of business the at hand. In the beginning Oscar tried to go into Robert's computer, but he didn't know the password for signing on, so he started using commonly used passwords, like birth dates, pets name, mother's maiden name, rarely used for this type of password, but trying it anyway, and he looked for a note pad with the password scribbled on it, but with no luck on this, that would be too easy, so he went in the back door of the operating system as he called it which I did not want to know what he was doing with that equipment he brought with him, probably not totally legal, but what do I know... After he got into the profile on Outlook the first thing on the e mail was the same picture that was in his room of what was emailed to him from another computer, but only signed as baby girl, who ever she was, but Oscar could find out what computer this was sent from by the name of the email provider, but would take some time. Most of the rest of it was spam which is a term for junk email and some emails from Regina wanting to see him and that was about it, but I wanted to get another look at that photo so he went back to it and there was something sticking out of his top pocket, but I couldn't make out what it was, maybe a piece of paper. Lillian asked me about the note she had found and turned over to me, but I was not ready to turn loose of it yet, so I asked her if I could keep it a little longer, and it was fine with her as long as I returned it. Oscar looked around the room a little more to see if he could come up with something I may have missed, but with no luck except some magazines on cars and half nude girls, which I am a little surprised his mom hadn't confiscated yet, but nothing else grabbed out at us that would help find Robert. I told Lillian I would like to talk with her a little more and she tried to think of something else that might help us on the case and she told me some of the places Robert used to go, like the garage in town close to their home and work on old cars with the owner Buddy, she said she had forgotten about that, but we could talk with him and see if maybe he had seen Robert close to the time he had went missing. Lillian was so anxious to hear anything on Robert that it was getting to her a little, she said. So Oscar and I decided to leave her alone awhile to get back her composure and maybe we would talk another time. Besides I wanted to head home after I stopped by

Buddy's garage, but Buddy had already gone for the day when we went by and the young man there working said to come back tomorrow, so I left my card and bid Oscar farewell and headed home to fix dinner for Ronnie and I.

But he was not in yet and I thought I was late. I took a couple of chicken breasts out of the freezer and micro'ed them for a few minutes and then put them on the grill to smoke a bit and popped us each a potato in to bake and made a green salad and hot French bread and had a nice peaceful dinner with a glass of wine to top it off. I told Ronnie about the kind of day I had and what I had learned, such as it was, but Ronnie was too busy telling me about things happening at work for him, about trying to make deadlines on engine orders and delivery dates on them way up to 2010 which was very discouraging. This is one of the reasons I retired from the same place that he works at. Nothing ever went the way it was supposed to and customers cursing at you and the boss throwing fits because the phones were not getting answered, but heaven forbid if they would have to hire more help. My job was inside sales most of the twenty years I was there. I got kind of burned out there and disgusted with the whole job scene, they would send you to customer service seminars to be courteous and helpful to customers and then new management came in, and all that went out the window. You were supposed to bend over backward to please your customer, but then they started telling us that didn't matter any longer that he couldn't buy this material anywhere else and it got so bad I just had enough one day and walked out and went home and called and quit and asked for retirement. So here I am working as a gumshoe as they used to call us, but at least I'm my own boss. I think Ronnie and I are a lot happier anyway, I don't come home crying and mad as an old hen and have a lot more time to see my grandkids and be there for them if they need me.

CHAPTER 10

The next morning I got up to another hot one, about 90 and rising and went for my morning walk after I had my coffee, then I drove down town to look at some offices for rent in a business complex which is not saying much in size especially, but what do you expect for a small town like ours. I had been thinking about renting something so I could get my files and boxes of some of my old cases out of my house. Since I had opened my investigating business almost a year ago officially, I had been working out of my home, and it was getting a little crowded, but now I think I am ready to expand and broaden my horizons, and see how it goes. The lady from the real estate office was waiting for me when I drove up, and was a bit pushy, but said the owner wanted to lease out the entire complex, and it was harder to lease out the spaces than he thought it was going to be, when he had them built, as an investment, of course, but after all, this is a relatively small town. She went on to show me the office at the end of the complex, which was the smallest one and was very compact, or you could say it was small but I thought would do nicely. By the time I moved my old desk and chair and file cabinets in and maybe a plant or two and a coffee pot, that will just about be all the space I'll have. But I can make it work for now if the money is right, since I will never get rich at this but can make a decent living if the cases keep dribbling in like they have been so far. I would probably have more work if I took all the divorce cases of following spouses around trying to gather up all the dirt on them, but I have to space those out so I don't get hostile myself. After the last one I worked on I didn't speak a decent word to Ronnie for a week, so he ordered me not to take another one. But I don't take orders too well, so I kind of pick and choose some of those cases for the experience and it helps pay the bills.

I told the real estate lady that I would take the office if the price was good enough for me to make the lease every six months and she assured me it was, but she is in it to make a profit for her and her client. But I don't think I could get a better deal here for what I was wanting, so I paid six months for the lease in advance. Maybe I would be here for at least that long. That evening I started moving in and called the phone company and all the other utilities and Ronnie got off a little early so he could help and see the place. He brought a bottle of white wine and a pizza and we celebrated on the floor, since I had forgotten to bring an extra chair for clients to sit on, but it was cozy and I went back and got the chair and a small loveseat we had from another set of furniture we had quit using a few years ago, which I get tired of things easily and want to change every so often. Well the next thing I need to do is put an answering machine in on the phone, since I won't be here a lot of the time and may be expanding and a secretary will come later, but now I will have to solo it. The office had more room in it than I thought, and still looked a little bare but I'm sure I will fill it up later. For now I had to use the bathroom for getting water for the coffee pot and use one of the built-in counter desk tops to set it on but it was my first office and I would make it work out great, you have to be optimistic. So Ronnie and I went home that night dog tired but very satisfied with ourselves at the accomplishment of the day.

When we went in the telephone voicemail was flashing so I checked to see who had called and it was my sister Ladonna calling to see if Ronnie and I wanted to meet her and Arnie for drinks and dinner tomorrow night and just checking to see what we were doing, but it was too late to call her back tonight so I made myself a note to call her back in the morning first thing before going to the office. There was another message from a Mr. Dodd from the local high school that said he wanted to talk to me about Robert Chambers and an incident at school just before Robert disappeared, and to please call him at his break at ten in the morning, Hmm, this may be the break I am looking for. Well, the end of the messages, so it’s just about time for lights out, and I think Ronnie's are already out, didn't hear him stirring at all now.

Something woke me about 2:00 A.M. and I saw a light coming from the living room so I woke Ronnie and he went to see what was going on, and then I heard a loud thump and got scared and screamed and called 911, then I just had to make sure Ronnie was ok. He was standing with a baseball bat that one of the grandkids had left that we kept behind the door. He said someone jumped out the window that we must have left unlocked, that when I screamed the culprit ran. Ronnie and I looked around to see if anything was missing, and the only thing disturbed was some bills and other papers on the desk in the living room, so they were looking for something, Ronnie said, and if it was something on your case then they didn't know you had moved everything concerning all your cases down to the office building. You are right, I'm getting too close to something that someone does not want me to find out and this gives me an eerie feeling that Robert is not going to show up safe and sound. Ronnie and I waited up for the Sheriff's Dept. to show up which this time only took twenty minutes, which was a far cry from the four hours it took them when we were broken into three years ago. The deputy asked me if we had made any new enemies lately and I told him what I do and he naturally associated the break-in with an angry client, which I think was an excuse because they can't do much after the fact, so they said to check and see what we were missing, which any idiot would have already done. I decided to look through things in the dining room which is adjoining the room where the desk is, and looked around a bit, but saw nothing out of place. Ronnie and I didn't sleep much the rest of the night, worrying about what had happened and, if I am getting close then we will have to be very careful about our surroundings and security for the house, so we agreed to call an alarm company in town tomorrow before I leave for the office. And maybe this will deter them from any further intrusion, or at least make it harder for them to get in. Probably, if we had a dog it would help but neither one of us is an animal lover, so that's out for now but we are leaving all options open. The clock went off at 5:00 A.M. and seemed that we had just gotten back to sleep. But we both drug out of bed very tired and I just couldn't think of staying in the house alone, after he went to work, so I called Ladonna, and Arnie was up getting ready to leave for the station, so I went over and crashed on their couch, and Ladonna went back over to the house with me to get ready for work. I took her on over with me to see the new office and we got into an interesting conversation about her working with me or for me in a round about way. She said that she could be here at the office when I was out on the road a few hours a day and do some light work such as answering phones and paying the bills and answering mail, which I never thought of myself as having a secretary and I wouldn't have a lot for her to do right now, until business was a little better. So I agreed to give her the job any way, she is very persuasive, but hoping it wouldn't come back to bite me, at a later date, but only part time. Yeah right, as pushy as she is, it will be full time. Now my sister and I are not the closest but can tolerate each other, most of the time, hope this works without having a murder on our hands and so I took her back home by way of the donut shop around the corner, for kolaches and coffee, might be a while before I get anything else. In the meantime Arnie was going to do some checking on the incident at our house last night and get back to me.

Chapter 11

I went by the school to talk to Mr. Dodd that morning, hopefully he would add something helpful to what I had already uncovered. Mr. Dodd looked more like a college professor than a high school teacher, with a yellow vest and green shirt and khaki Dockers and a yellow tie with big polka dots along with Nikes, boy what a fashion statement he was trying to make but I was not real sure what kind. I asked Mr. Dodd what he had for me about Robert and he went on to tell me that just before Robert disappeared an older model blue truck came around and the driver called him out of the crowd of friends that he was with. There is that blue truck again. I was walking across campus just in time to hear the driver, he said, which was an older man, which he didn't get a good look at him but, he could tell by the tone of the voice that he was older, and that he sounded a little angry. Robert was yelling something at him and the man was cursing him, as I got closer the argument got louder and louder and all I could determine from the conversation was that there was another person the man was referring to, but I didn't hear a name mentioned, and that it was a girl they were arguing about and the man threatened to take care of him if he didn't keep his distance from the girl. Robert just brushed him off and walked away from the truck, but the person nearly ran him down as he pulled away. Well, Robert seemed a little shaken up and I asked him what it was all about and he just waved me off, and with these kids you can't really push too hard because of all the rules the school system has, it goes into harassment, and then you surely create more problems. Some teachers have been summoned in by the school board for just trying to help one of these kids, so it is a very thin line there on what we can do for them, but it still does not keep us from trying, and if we help one child then it is an accomplishment for our system and shows that it is working. I asked Mr. Dodd if any of the others in the group knew what was going on and he said he did question a few of them, but they clammed up tighter than a drum, no one wants to get involved. And heaven forbid if they would rat out a friend. The kids were beginning to flock in now to the classroom so he said he had to get back and deal with all the camaraderie in there, so I told him I really appreciated the time he had given me and that if he thought of anything helpful to please give me a call and left him my card. I stopped and called Ladonna to see if there were any messages, since I had used my same number from my home office everything should carry on over to the office. Ladonna said there was a message from my darling grandson Jonathon, I think she was being kind of snidey when she said it, but I tried to ignore her and carry on with business. He wanted to know if I was coming out to his house soon, needs gas money, I guess, but giving him the benefit of the doubt. After all he is a struggling teen-ager, so I called him back and he just wanted me to visit with him, imagine that, but he does that sometime. I told him I would be out there on the weekend and this was only Tuesday, but he was satisfied with that. So Ladonna went on to tell me that Arnie called and said he would be over to see me this afternoon, so to hang around if I could work him in ten minutes, he wanted to give me some information about the break-in last night. Ronnie had left a message that he was just checking on me after the bad night we had and to return his call when I had a free moment.

Ladonna said that was all the messages and she was about to go find her something for lunch, did I want her to bring me something, no, but maybe a diet drink would do me for now. Ladonna had arranged things pretty efficient so her desk would be handy for her and get everything in here that we needed. I already had a fax machine and copier so we set it up and she was already making good use of them. Huh, this might just work, I have no complaints yet, but after all it is just the first day, anything can happen, all right Suzy, you and your evil mind. I called Ronnie back to assure him that I was fine this morning and hoped he was the same but that I still felt a little skittish about someone prowling around in our house and that I need to call an alarm company. Ronnie said he was already checking on it, not to worry so much, but he knows I'm going to anyway, just my nature I guess. Arnie came by about two in the afternoon and said that there had not been any other disturbances in our area so it was an isolated incident and to take all precautions, and maybe have a gun close but they probably would not come back, but no guarantees, boy that's real comforting. What are the chances that they will try to come here and check my files if they didn't find what they were looking for, and he said, it was a pretty good chance, did I have any security here? Yes, I told him, there is a private service that drives around and checks things every so often, but I'm not familiar with him since I just moved in here, but I will make it a point to meet with him today and kind of size him up, I will let you know what I think of him. Arnie asked, also, since there aren't any close neighbors, is there any one that could drive by and check on things every once in a while? I think I can talk Mandy into checking on the house, I said, it will give her something to do, which she stays pretty busy anyway, but we try to look out for each other. He also asked if I had any idea what they could have been looking for and the only thing I could think of was the letter Lillian had given me, but why would anyone be interested in that, since there was nothing in it, really. And that was in my purse, but they didn't have a chance to come in to our bedroom, I always take my purse in there at night, just a dumb old habit, but maybe not so dumb.

Arnie looked in the letter and didn't get much out of it either, and said; "I take it you don't know who wrote this, so maybe it wasn't that."

I shook my head no and said, "Not a clue. They had to be searching for something concerning the case, but I'm stumped at this moment, but maybe they will show their hand again."

Arnie left and I went to talk to security, about what their routine is at night and about my home break in. He seemed pretty confident that he could handle an intruder if need be, so I hope he is right. I needed to check on another case of mine that I had neglected lately with some animals disappearing from a private shelter here in town, after the camera was installed it kind of slowed whoever the guilty one was down a bit, but still having animals missing, but not as often. I suspect an inside job but no proof to really go on. I needed to go out to one of the employee's residences and check around while he was not there, so this was as good of a time as any, I suppose. I had gotten the address from the owner and this was the only one I hadn't checked, but I don't expect a thief to keep the goods close to home, but you never know. When I drove up it was too quiet for noisy animals so I just looked around a little on the outside, with no luck, so I decided to go inside with my trusty hairpin that I keep in my purse and I let myself in the back door not to draw any attention from some nosy neighbor. This place was messier than my house usually is and needed a woman's touch, but there was no short supply of magazines and not the kind I would like my grandkids to see, but I wouldn't put it past them, especially the two oldest ones. There was a stack of papers on the dresser and a statement for a warehouse rental in downtown Houston, wonder what he has in a warehouse, little furry mongrels, I hope, but that would be too easy, but worth a try, well I will call Arnie and have him check it out maybe we will get lucky, sure would like to wrap this one up and collect. So I made a call to Arnie and lo and behold when I got home the phone was ringing and it was Arnie, to let me know that I was right about the warehouse and they retrieved most of the animals, so I called the owner of the shelter and told him they were being returned to them. Now if I could just figure out what happened to Robert, but I didn't think it was going to be that easy. Well, the heat started to let up a little as time went by but I still hadn't solved the Chambers case, although I still worked on it and Lillian said she had been waiting on news of her son, over a year, so she could wait a little longer. I have never given up on a case and I was not about to start now. I did give it a rest, so I could see if things would settle down and there were no more problems with burglars so far, so that tells me someone was trying to scare me off the case, but it's not going to work. It was the end of October and we were getting ready for Thanksgiving but not really looking forward to this one, last year my two oldest grandsons got in to a heated argument, no, not really an argument but a knockdown fight in the living room floor, Ronnie Jr. and Ronnie Sr. had to pull them apart, Jonathon the youngest of the two is about a head taller than his brother Dirk and just about got the best of him and Dirk was surprised. He seemed to learn his lesson and has backed off intimidating Jonathon as much as he used to. Jonathon can be very irritating and annoying when he wants to, but hopefully they will both grow out of their aggravations to each other.

Chapter 12

got up to another cool and beautiful day, boy I'm sure glad it cooled down, because the fall is a great time of year when the leaves start falling, and going out for my morning walk is a pleasure, so I stayed out as long as I could and still get a days work in. I went home and had my shower and had a couple more cups of coffee and called my friend Mandy to check on her and she wanted me to go have breakfast with her so I had to hurry out the door, but I heard the phone ringing just as I pulled the door shut so I had to turn off the alarm and grab it before it stopped. It was Ladonna with a message to call a Mrs. Lane when I got the chance and I said I would as soon as I could. Mandy and I went to IHOP, her favorite place for breakfast and I have to admit she is right, but with all those choices, there goes my waistline, what's left of it, can hardly see it any more. The place was full and we had to wait in line a bit but well worth the wait, so we caught up on what we had both been up to and talked about organizing the quilt group again, which I enjoy so much, when I can work it in to my schedule, mostly chatting with the others and just plain enjoying the gossip, but we will wait until after all the holidays are over and hope I have the time. Mandy said she was also getting ready for the holidays as it is her favorite time of the year also, and she was cooking Thanksgiving for family and having Christmas at her sons. I thanked her for watching over our house while we were at work during the summer months.

"I don't mind Suzy, but why don't you think about getting a dog,"

I declined to even discuss it, so we finished our coffee and went our separate ways. My first stop after that was the office to see if Ladonna had anything else for me, but she roped me into a conversation about what I was having for Thanksgiving, which I was not sure why, she usually doesn't care enough to ask, because they always went to Arnie's folks in Tennessee, so me and my big mouth, in went my foot to ask about their plans and they decided to stay here for Thanksgiving and so I had to ask if they would like to come over for lunch and she said yes. So to thicken the pot I asked why they were not going out of town and opened a long story which I didn't stay for all of it. Something about a family feud with Arnie's sister, so I left it alone, but first I called Mrs. Lane to see if she would be home, and made my way over there by way of Main street and the traffic was beginning to pickup ,so I tried the back way and that helped tremendously. I called Oscar, for the first time in a while just to check on him and invite him over for Sunday dinner and he asked if he could bring a friend, which I hesitated a short moment but decided to tell him ok. Now this is a first, must be serious, wonder who it is, but probably won't know him or her anyway, there goes my evil suspicious mind again. When I reached Mrs. Lanes house, which seemed a long drive, she answered right away. She asked if I wanted coffee or something and I declined but did have a dry mouth so I reconsidered and she got me a coke, and when she came back in I asked her what was the problem?

"I was wondering if you had any word on Robert yet, that Sabrina is very unhappy these days and I thought after this much time lapsed she would have moved on, but she seems to really be angry with him and I am not sure why. Maybe if you talk to her and get her to open up to you, since you were on the case to begin with, but I didn't know if you still were."

"Yes I am still working on it and have no intentions of quitting until I get some answers but if I uncover something that will help the police in finding Robert, you know that I will have to turn it over to them."

"I know", she said, "but she needs to talk and I don't know if a therapist would be the answer and if you talk to her and think she needs professional help then I will provide her with one. I am really concerned for her and think she has an idea that Robert was seeing someone behind her back but won't say who it is and how she knows, but if she did talk to you it may help you also to get more information. Sabrina used to be close friends with Regina next door but she has dropped most of her friends and doesn't go out much."

"I will try", I told her "but nothing is sure." and she said she would be in from school later this afternoon, if I wanted to come back then. I told her I would return later, and headed for my next appointment, which was to meet Oscar downtown for lunch at a place called La Masada which was a combination deli and cafe. The waitress was a little too anxious to wait on us, which is very different, but welcomed for a change. Oscar got there about the same time I did, punctual and impressive, I figured he would be late as usual, but boy was I wrong. So the waitress seated us at the other end of the building and apologized for all the noise, but after all it was my choice so why was she sorry. I ordered a half of a ham and cheese club sandwich and a cup of baked potato soup and Oscar made a big deal of ordering a salad to show me up for watching his waistline, but didn't faze me in the least, but then he topped it off with a big piece of apple pie and ice cream, some big weight watcher, huh, I said, and he just sat there and glared at me. Oscar said he was trying to talk to some of Jesse Daniels relatives, but that they didn't want to open up much to him, and that His uncle Mort was very uncooperative. Mort was trying to sound like a good old boy gone bad and he did let Jesse live with him, but only as a favor to his dad, and the boy never was any good, in his words, always causing him trouble. But Mort never would go into details of what all had happened, like he was hiding something and acted like it was a burden for him to let Jesse stay with him, even temporarily. I think I will do some checking on good old uncle Mort, find out if there are any skeletons in that closet, I get the idea that there is more to Uncle Mort than meets the eye. Jesse did get into some trouble when he was younger, but the records are sealed, because he was too young, so we will probably hit a dead end there.

"Oscar, to change the subject now, who is this mystery person you are bringing to our house Sunday?"

"I'd rather not say, but you will find it very interesting."

"Yeah that's what I'm afraid of." But I left it at that and finished up my tea and left. I kind of toyed with the idea of Robert and Jesse running off together, but remembered what Lillian had said about knowing in her heart that he wouldn't run away, and if she was that close to him, I really feel bad for her and am not giving up without a fight, to find out what really happened to him. On my way home I had to make a quick run by the cleaners to pick up Ronnie's suit for an awards dinner he and I had to make an appearance at, this was his thirty year award from the company and is quite an honor, I think, but Ronnie doesn't seem too excited over it, so I have to be for the both of us. I just kept trying to not let my mind wonder to the fact that something had happened to both of those boys, but resigned to the fact that it was very possible and probable but I would cross that bridge when I came to it.

Chapter 13

When I got home there were two messages, but I was not in the mood to check them at this time so I ignored it and went and put my feet up for a while, and guess I dozed off because the phone woke me up and it was Mrs. Lane calling to see if I had forgotten that I was supposed to come and talk to Sabrina, and I had to tell her that I had fallen asleep and if it was ok I would make it tomorrow evening. Well, I meandered into the kitchen to see what I could take out of the freezer for dinner since Ronnie was not home yet, wonder what's keeping him, then I remembered I didn't listen to the phone messages. They were both from Ronnie telling me he would be kind of late and for me not to fix dinner, that they were taking a co-worker out for his birthday. Well I think I will just see if I can get a little done on my case, since I brought some of the paper work home with me and I needed to go over it a little, and maybe if I read some more on it something may jump out at me that I missed. Well no such luck, so I just got back in my chair and went back to sleep, when I heard a noise out in the front yard, and we are plagued with possum and armadillo under the house, but with the prowler we had before I was a little startled. I went to look out the blinds when I heard the key in the door and it was Ronnie, a little tipsy.

"You scared me half to death." I said, and he just kind of looked at me with a blank stare, and grinned, and I knew he was wasted, big time, so I led him into the bedroom and put him to bed and returned to the living room, because I still wasn't very sleepy. I washed a few dishes that weren't crawling yet and straightened up a little and then decided to take a shower, that usually puts me out but no luck this time, so I tossed and turned until about 2 A.M. and finally went to sleep. The next morning Ronnie was a little hung over and didn't have too much to say, but I did get some coffee down him and a piece of toast and we talked a little about my headway on things, which didn't take long, because there wasn't very much of that. Then I decided to go see Lillian before she went to work, but I don't really know what I thought I was going to find, but it won't hurt to see if I can get a few more leads, because at this point I was at a loss as to where to look next. Lillian's house was a large brick house and had a big wood fence around it and when I pulled into the driveway there was a familiar truck parked there, which I recognized as Oscars, so this was the friend he was bringing to the house Sunday, I should have guessed that one, but it went completely over my head.

When I went in Oscar was sitting on the couch drinking a cup of coffee, and I'm thinking, did I tell him I was coming over here this morning, but then I remembered that I decided at the last moment that I would go see Lillian, but Oscar was sitting there without a shirt and shoes, so duh, how dumb am I? Oscar sort of grinned at me when I looked his way, kind of like Ronnie had when he came in a little inebriated last night, but Oscar was not drunk this early, so I just grinned back and sat down and tried to regain my composure. I explained to Lillian that I was looking for new leads in the case, but I was not sure of exactly what, so to bear with me.

Oscar said, "Would you like me to bow out of this investigation, since I am a little too close to it personally, or do you think I can be objective enough, that I will not let personal get involved with business, and you know me well enough to know me better than that."

"Oscar", I said, "we have known each other long enough that I think you can keep your personal feelings separated from the daily routine of the case, so we will leave it alone for now, but if at any time either I or Lillian thinks there is a conflict of interest then you will be off the case. Is it understood?"

"Yes, that will work for me." he said and Lillian shook her head yes, in response. "Ok, so let's get down to the business at hand, and I need to know some of what we have already discussed and see if you can think of something to add. Do you think Robert was unhappy or upset at the time about something or maybe preoccupied and did he mention anyone else that he knew that may have a problem in school or socially, just anything that may help?"

"I can't think of anything, but all kids think they are pressured with just everyday life and school, and I'm sure he wasn't any different but Robert was not in the habit of telling me much, we were close in some ways but, you know how teens are, they just tell you what they think you want to hear."

I said, "I hear ya, that's pretty much what I discovered raising my two. Can you think of anyone he might confide in concerning his problems at school if there were any?" I asked.

"No," she said, "maybe Sabrina, but he shouldn't have had any real problems at 17 years old, you'd think."

"Well, I am going over to Sabrina's this afternoon and give it another shot at talking to her, but she seems real uptight lately, so I don't know how that will go." Lillian showed me some of Robert's school work from last year and he seemed to be a pretty good student. Lillian got up and went into the kitchen for more coffee and Oscar looked over at me and asked me why I was going over old information I had already gotten from her, and I said, “I just wanted to refresh my memory and see if anything had changed.”

Oscar winked at me and said, “Hey Suzy this is Oscar you are talking to, not some amateur, what’s really going on?" and I told him that I wanted to start opening old wounds with the neighbors, but just one at a time and see if the harassment toward me started again so I could narrow it down to who was behind it.

“Someone does not want us snooping, but you are barking up the wrong tree with Lillian”, he said, “she worships that boy, and like all parents, thinks he can do no wrong, but still in the back of her mind she thinks something or someone or both caused him to disappear and that maybe he is not the perfect child she thought she had raised.” and we really don't like to but sometimes all parents think that way in my opinion and I said you might be right. When they are away from home, they are still responsible for their own actions. We can't be with them twenty four hours a day and at some point we have to trust them. We really don't like to think about that, but sometimes all parents think that way in my opinion and I said he might be right, but to keep his ears open without breaking her trust or actually spying on her, and he shook his head ok.

“Oscar, do you think we will really find this kid alive, and unharmed, after this long of a time, you know the odds are not very good? This is really preying on my mind heavily and maybe you should try to prepare Lillian for the worst even if it never comes to that.”

Oscar said, :Yeah I have considered it and I hear ya, but I hate to take her hope that he is alive away too soon since we don't really know anything for sure, that’s the reason I have been sticking close to her, well one reason." and he winked "and we do really enjoy each other's company. We laugh a lot, which I think she needs that right now, and we go out a lot and she is a wonderful cook." but I said that's coming from a man that sits in front of the boob tube and eats cold Spaghetti- O's straight out of a can.

"But you two do seem to click with each other", I said, "and you seem like you have a great thing going for you, and that's a plus. Would you like to go over with me and see Sabrina this afternoon or do you have a full day ahead? You could keep Mrs. Lane busy while I kind of work on Sabrina."

Oscar nodded yes, I have the feeling she knows more than she is saying but afraid to say too much. She is young and has a very nice home and seems to have an abundance of everything a teen would want and this is a great time in her life and has everything going for her yet she is still in a funk, what's up with that? But my grandkids always want something more, guess no one is ever satisfied but if you think about it kids are really under a lot of peer pressure and they think they have to keep up with all the other kids, designer clothes, fast and lifted up trucks, best looking boyfriend or girlfriend, take Jonathon for example his truck is up so high in the air with big tires and a lift kit that I have to get a step stool to get up in it and then I still get a nose bleed.

I looked out the window of the living room and it was beginning to rain, a slow drizzle and wind blowing, and looked like it was getting colder outside, which the weather man did say we were in for a cool front coming in today at midday, but do they really know? I kind of spaced out for a moment to check the weather and when I revived myself, Oscar and Lillian were talking about the evening ahead and what they were planning. Boy, I'm glad I'm not dating and trying to impress anyone, but you never stop working at marriage either, so it's no different with Ronnie and me, just a little more relaxed. Lillian brought more coffee and set it in front of me which I hadn't noticed until Oscar pointed it out to me, but I felt like I'd had just about enough so I tried to get back in the conversation, and business.

"You do not have any relatives at all, that Robert might have called or got in touch with?" I asked Lillian.

"No", she said, "I had an old aunt in Mississippi but I don't know if she is even still alive." she answered with a screwed up look on her face, "and I wouldn't know how to get in touch with her if I chose to. I will see if I still have her last known address if it will help at all."

"I don't know, but it's worth a try to check out any lead, maybe he went through there at some point." Down deep I didn't really think so, but wouldn't tell her that. It must have been rough on Robert not to have any relatives to be close to, like, grandparents or distant cousins or someone to be in touch with, and she just shook her head yes. She said after her husband passed away it would have been nice to have someone, but that's the way life is sometime and you just accept the way things are and go on with your life. I was beginning to feel real bad for her, since her son really was all she had and a hand full of friends and those were mostly co-workers. What a life this must be, and got me to thinking about my own family, think I will try to call Ronnie when I leave here. It almost made me appreciate having even Ladonna, but not quite. But maybe if I just hear Ronnie's voice and see if he might have lunch with me, it might pull me out of this longing for family mood. Well we wrapped up the meeting there and I went back to town to check in with Ladonna at the office and to make some phone calls. Ladonna most certainly surprised me with the way she took charge of the office and is running things, she never took charge of anything, not even her own life, and if not for Arnie she wouldn't have picked up the pieces of her own life after her nasty divorce, but she has surely surprised me with this responsibility she has taken on. It frees me up for all the running around I have to do and keeps me from making so many trips home to do all the paper work involved and returning phone calls. Which reminds me, I think I will get me a cell phone, since Ronnie has been bugging me so adamantly lately and he has one, but I hate to think that the kids and grandkids will be able to reach me even when I'm on the road, then I really will never have any time of my own. Oh well, the price you pay for having a family, but I wouldn't trade it for anything. I am always being told that I am too close to my family, but I think there is no such thing, and maybe I stick my nose in sometime when I shouldn't, but when I do, they tell me instantly, which is very seldom. And the older grandsons just don't answer the telephones when I call them if they don't want to talk to me, which makes me a little angry, but they have their own lives.

Chapter 14

I met Oscar at the Lanes' to speak with Sabrina in the afternoon, and the weather was getting very nasty out, also this was my second trip today out in this area which was a good ways from my home. Sabrina was not too happy to see me as usual but I just had to try again with her, it may help the both of us, to talk about things, as I was feeling kind of isolated from my family, but really wasn't. She sat with me out in the den while Oscar and Mrs. Lane got acquainted and talked about what kind of neighbors were around them.

I asked Sabrina, "How is school going, and are you going to graduate?"

"Yeah, I hope so but my senior year is sure a lot harder than I expected, but I will make it by the skin of my teeth."

I asked, "Would Robert have also graduated this year?" And that was the wrong thing to ask, because she all but went ballistic on me. "Why does everyone keep badgering me about Robert, we were not even that close any more since...", then she caught herself, but it was too late to stop now.

"Since what Sabrina?" I asked.

She started to cry uncontrollably and looked away as if she were a million miles away, but I was trying to keep her talking, to maybe find out something more, and she looked me straight in the eye and said, "Since I caught him with someone else. I was furious, but I still don't know what happened to him. I really feel guilty because I cursed him and her out just before he came up missing and I don't speak to her any longer and never will."

I asked, "Who are you talking about, who did you catch Robert with?" but she turned away and did not answer me.

"I have to know if maybe he ran away with her and what to tell poor Lillian, she is about out of her mind with worry. Now who are you referring to that he was seeing beside you?"

She said, "He didn't run away with her because I see her all the time, just go right next door and you can talk to her all you want."

“You mean Regina?” She nodded her head yes and cried harder and went on to tell me that they had been friends all their life and gone to the same school forever or so it seemed and that she couldn't believe that she would do this to her, but that Regina said when she came back from living with her grandmother, she and Robert became involved and that neither one of them meant to hurt her, but it just happened.

“Regina was living with her grandmother at some point?” I asked.

She nodded yes and said that her dad sort of went into a slump when her mother died and he didn't want her living with her brother Alton, who was older from his first marriage, so he carted her off to her grandmother, which at first she didn't want to go but finally gave in, and didn't really have a choice, when he puts his foot down that’s it, there’s no talking to him, Regina always said. I pulled out my little notebook and started taking notes, and a fast notation to check up on older brother and why her dad didn't trust him to take care of his younger sister.

Well, we are finally getting somewhere, hopefully, and I turned to Sabrina with my serious face and asked, "Why didn't you tell me all of this before, it could have saved me and a lot of people a whole lot of grief and especially you, but don't let all of this get to you so badly as you are doing, because sweetheart, you have your whole life ahead of you and you are too young and outgoing to be so serious about anything except for getting out of high school and going to college, by the way where were you wanting to go to college next fall?"

"I am either kicking around Sam Houston State, or A&M, they're both great colleges and was looking forward to living on campus with people that I don't know or them me." she said.

"That will give you a fresh start and you will be great, you seem to be such a serious and conscientious person but you have to forget all this and concentrate on your future. I know your mom is proud of you, and I also know we parents do not always give you kiddos the credit and praise that we should but everyone gets so caught up in their own lives they just don't think, so you hang in there."

Sabrina gave me a half smile and a thumbs up so maybe she will be ok, but it will be a rough road for her for a while. She proceeded to tell me that she knew something was wrong when Robert quit coming around and when he did he was preoccupied about something.

"Did he mention any trouble he might have been in?"

"No," she said, "but I know there was some reason he quit going to the garage where he liked to hang out, because he wouldn't even look that direction when we passed, but I never did know what had happened there. Mrs. Lighter, I think I missed my best friend Ginny more than I did him, now isn't that silly."

I looked surprised I suppose, because she asked, "What is it?"

"What did you call her just now?"

She said, "You mean Ginny, that's what I always

called her since kindergarten, its short for Regina and was easier for me to remember when we were little. Does that mean something?" she asked. And I proceeded to tell her about the letter we had found in Robert's room signed G. So it was from Regina. "I don't want to get her in any trouble, because I really do want her for a friend still, and will call her later to try and straighten this mess out. Ginny and I had planned to go to the same college and be roommates on campus, and then maybe, rent an apartment off campus our second year, and it's been over a year since we have talked, she may not even talk to me, but I will give it a try."

So I gave her a thumbs-up and tried to assure her that things would work out for the two of them in time, that this would all pass. I was not sure I believed it either, but what else could I say? We then returned to the living room where her mom and Oscar had a weird conversation going about the different types of people he had to deal with, and Mrs. Lane seemed to take it all in with a grain of salt, but seemed not to understand what he was talking about and he just rolled his eyes at me when she turned to Sabrina to make sure she was all right. I just smiled his way and waved him to come on, so we could leave.

The weather was getting horrible and I was ready to get in before it was too bad, but I had a couple of stops to make first. I wanted to stop and check on Ronnie Jr. and Brent, I still worry about them. He is a single parent and I have to say an excellent one at that, but you always want to know their life is going smooth, which they still meet a lot of new challenges every day. I know Brent still misses his Mom every day when he doesn't get to see her, but it was his choice, of course, to live with his Dad. It is a terrible thing that he and his ex cannot even talk without fighting or cursing with one another. Ronnie Jr. is very bitter toward her and she despises him. After I left there I was going over the information Sabrina had given me in my mind, and it was a surprise to know that G. was Regina, but she did seem very up tight when I interviewed her and sort of clammed up when I asked her about Robert. Maybe there is more than meets the eye there, but I will have to handle it very carefully so I don't move too quickly and give someone a chance to come after me again. I will have to watch my back all the time now, when I start digging deeper into everything. I think I will call Arnie when I get home so he knows that I have new information and see if he can do some checking on the older brother of Regina's and a background check on the dad to see if there are any skeletons in that closet, and what happened to the first wife.

I didn't really have my mind on my driving when I went right into the rear end of another car, and the driver jumped out and started immediately yelling and cursing at me, and I guess I did the wrong thing in my reaction of it all, I just started laughing at him as loud as I could, just trying to lighten the moment, and he got so mad that he belted me right in the eye. What a big mistake, on his part, and I know there was fire in my eyes and I doubled my fist as my first thought but I calmly went back to my car and got my purse with my pistol in it and was ready to blow his foot off, when he started backing off and he almost started to cry. Just as I put the gun back in my purse an officer from the sheriff's department showed up and he proceeded to tell him that I pulled a gun on him and we both got hauled off to jail, him for hitting me and resisting arrest and me for carrying a concealed weapon and no permit, which I have one but just not with me, and I guess I have a dishonest face because they didn't believe me. So, what a great way to end a nasty day, my butt in jail, and you know the worst part is that I had to sit there until I could track down Ronnie which with one phone call and having to leave a message for him, and by the time he got it, it was starting to get dark out and the prostitutes were beginning to be hauled in and the place was filling up, so we decided we had a lot more in common than you would think. They were raising kids and grandkids, just like I was and some of these old girls were older than me, boy isn't that a kicker, and the dough they're bringing in, made me think I'm in the wrong business. It looked like we were in the same boat anyway both in jail. But, I'm afraid if I had to do that for a living I would surely starve to death. Ronnie finally made it to bail me out and brought my permit with him and when he found out how much the impound fee was he was ready to send me back to jail. By the time I got home my eye was blacker than the ace of spades and almost swelled closed. Ronnie got me a steak out of the freezer and put it on and said something about that was the way to take the swelling out, but I told him I'd rather be eating the steak, and then he looked at me and asked what door I ran into. I explained that the guy had hit me as soon as he got out just because when he started yelling at me I was going to try to make the best of it by laughing it off, but it just made him very angry, and he came at me with his fist. Ronnie became so angry that he called Arnie and told him what had happened and he didn't think it was right the way it was handled, because after all I had a permit for the gun, just not with me, which wasn't too bright, and an investigators license, and was protecting myself. I think Ronnie was as mad as I was and kicking the chair out of the way and yelling at no one in particular, but just blowing off steam. So he came out and took my statement and said nice shiner, and told me to come down and file on him and told me to hold my temper and not threaten the officer on duty.

He said, "I know how you are Suzy, I'm surprised you didn't shoot him." This evening had been a total disaster and I was ready to just run off and soak my head at the nearest bar, and I'm not a big drinker, but I think I would have made an exception on this one, but the way my luck was running today I would probably end up in the slammer with a drunk and disorderly charge. So I opted out to head for bed instead, after we got back from the jail house. Boy, maybe tomorrow will be better I thought as I stumped my big toe on the end table on the way to bed.

Chapter 15

The house had an awful chill in it when I got up, and my face felt and looked like a Mack truck had driven over it, my eye wouldn't open hardly at all, so I called Ladonna and told her I would be in later and she said, "Arnie told me what happened last night, you must have been really tired, or you sure have changed a lot, because ten years ago you would have shot him and told the police it was self defense. What's up? You mellowing out in your old age, Suze?"

"Ladonna, age has nothing to do with it, and I wish everyone would quit telling me I should have shot the guy, I am not that violent, it's just the guy caught me off guard and I didn't see it coming and you know me I don't get mad I get even."

"Uh oh, he is in for a big surprise I take it, well do not tell me anymore, I don't want in the middle of that. And I didn't say you should have shot him, I said I am shocked that you didn't."

About that time I heard Ronnie come into the room and he wanted to know what I intended to do, and to just leave it alone, but as he shook his head, he muttered something under his breath and looked me right in the eye, and asked, "I'm wasting my breath, aren't I?"

I just smiled and pecked him on the cheek and went and started the coffee. I sat down at the small table in the kitchen and had my coffee and looked at some of my notes from yesterday and was planning my next move and wondering where my camera was when the phone rang, and it was Ronnie's Mom telling me they were coming for Thanksgiving. Now, they are good people so this will be a nice surprise, but she went on to tell me they were going to stay for two weeks, so the first thing I thought of was that the house needed a complete face lift. Ronnie usually takes off that whole week so he can help me get everything ready for company. This will be a little different with Ladonna in the same room with Ronnie's mom, there's not much love there, but I will have to threaten Ladonna to keep her claws in. She tells you everything she's thinking and sometimes she doesn't do it in a nice way, and this may be one time when Ronnie will have second thoughts about taking his vacation. I told Ronnie who was on the phone and he didn't really have any reaction, that I could see except for groaning about having to unclutter the house which he does not like to clean and rake out things, we always end up throwing out things we want or need later, and saying things to each other that we ordinarily wouldn't think of saying, but that's the way it works. Ah, married life and family and so on.

I need to see if my guy I had the wreck with was released from jail last night on bail and find out where he lives and if he has a family, before I take my next step on this mess. If he is a family man I will leave it alone. But if not, boy, look out, and I'm betting he is not, he is just too arrogant, kids and spouse would have already nipped that in the bud, but we will see.

I kept going over in my mind what I had found out about Regina and her family and it didn't set too well with me, but I need to have a talk with the grandmother and I believe her home is not too far from me, so I can do that in the morning, since I am sporting this big shiner on my eye I think I will keep a low profile today and maybe make-up will cover a lot of it tomorrow better than today. I am sure glad the Houston quilt convention was last weekend and not this one, I probably would have had to pass it up. My next phone call was to Regina's house, but not to my surprise there was no answer so I didn't leave a message. I thought I would give it a try later, and then I called Oscar and asked, "What have you heard from Lillian, is there anything going on there?"

"No, except that she did get a phone call that she just kind of passed it off as an telemarketer, but she was on there a long time for that, so I will pursue it a little further and let you know, I really don't feel comfortable spying on her but we need all the help we can get at this point, so I tell myself that it is not spying and I think she knows it is all for the case, or at least I hope she sees it that way. Lillian is still holding out on hope that he is coming back to her, but I keep telling her the longer he is gone the less chance there is that he is still alive, just to prepare her for the worst, and Suzy, I do care a lot for her, and glad to have her in my life, and maybe I should back off and let you handle this one, but then if something happened to you because I am not there to watch your back then I wouldn't have a life anyway, because Ronnie would kill me. Which, I know you are a tough broad but this one has been so weird, with all the crazy things that have been happening, and you know as we get closer to the truth, you will be in a lot more danger, so I will stick with you through the end."

"I am afraid Robert's true colors will come out in the end, and maybe he is not the wonderful and innocent child she is wanting us to believe he is," I said, "but we still have to love our kids because that's the way we are molded into this life. It's all unconditional love even if we sense that they are not perfect, just because we say they are."

Oscar said, "There you go again, Suzy, you and your motherly ways coming out, but it does make a lot of sense, no matter how you word it or look at it. Suzy," he said, "what is the plan for Thanksgiving this year?" and I explained to him about all the family coming in and extended an invitation to him. But he said no thanks, Lillian had invited him over to her house and he wanted to watch some holiday football and have a peaceful and relaxing day, and he knew that with Ladonna there at our house it would not be a pretty sight. And in no way peaceful. I would have been offended if I had not agreed with him one hundred percent, so, I just loused around the rest of the day and Ronnie came home to check on me and stayed, which was very unusual, and I think he was not only worried about the eye but didn't comment on anything further, like maybe he thought someone would be following me again.

Chapter 16

Well the next morning the eye looked a lot better, so I had my coffee and made sure I had Regina's grandmother's address, and I went by the office to check on things there, but Ladonna was keeping things in pretty good order and had no messages but had a lot to babble about the eye and the incident. Oh well, what's new, she always has to put in her two cents, and as usual I just ignored her hoping she would go away, but fat chance of that happening.

"Suzy", she said, "How are things really going on the case and you are not going to talk to all these people again alone, are you? Arnie said it could get pretty bad if someone had really done something to Robert, and you could be right in the middle of things and you know I can go with you on some of these interviews, sometimes it is very slow here and I would like to get out some, so don't you have some field work for me to do, I believe that is what you call it, or does that sound silly?"

I just kind of shrugged and changed the subject and told her we needed to get a new chair and desk lamp for the office and she took the hint. But as I thought about it I got to thinking, maybe she could do some private snooping for some of the other clients we have. Well maybe that will come on down the road. Lord help us all turning my sister out onto the public, and before I left, I asked her to check on the guy that I ran into the other night. I gave her the information the police had given me, which was very little, and she just shook her head at me, and said she would take care of it.

I wanted to go and talk to Regina's grandmother and

ask her about Regina's mother and about this mysterious brother that no one seems to know very much about. There was a chill in the air and I didn't really dress for it, I thought it would warm up some, but it hasn't, and here the weather changes on a dime from hot to cold and back again. The traffic was picking up now and I was trying my best to get to Regina's grandmother's house before it got too late but it would probably be late before I got home so I stopped and called to tell Ronnie I would not be home for awhile, and listened to his speech about being careful and all that rot, but I am lucky he really still cares for me, after all of these years and all the complications of my job he has had to put up with. I just smiled real big at the thought of it.

Since the grandmother didn't live too far from us, I swung by and checked mail, grabbed a jacket, and picked up my camera and gun. If I didn't get to shoot someone with my gun then possibly I could shoot them with my camera, and also I made sure I had my gun permit, but I was seriously suspicious of everyone these days, even grandmothers, isn't that a kicker? Being a grandmother myself it's hard to imagine her to be even as mean as I am, but after my confrontation the other night I am not about to take any chances, grandmother or not.

Sabrina had said that the grandmother was always nice to her and that they were around her quite a bit before the mother died and that this was the maternal grandmother, but after the mother passed away, she did not see her often, and she never seemed to come over any more, which would seem strange unless she had good reason, but it must be a serious one to keep someone from their grandchild. But I'll bet anything it is not her idea, or maybe she has some suspicions of her own, and doesn't trust being at Regina's Dad's, so I will have to be very careful of the way I put my questions to her, and try not to intimidate her in any way. That is so easy to do with a stranger if you are not careful, because usually they are nervous at first. The way I am thinking so much about it, I don't think she is the only one nervous here. On my way to the grandmother's house I had a second thought about bringing up Regina's brother right away and was wondering why no one else knew much about him, but I would soon find out, and maybe get a picture of him, and some input about what kind of person he is, and so on. Traffic seemed very heavy now, but I took the back way so I don't have to get on the belt-way , it's always busy, but not as bad as the freeway, the only thing is, you have to drop your speed to 55 mph and it takes longer, always a trade off somewhere. I kicked up my heater and slowed up with the rest of the motorists, sure seemed to be getting colder if you can believe that. Or maybe my car heater is on the blink again, and I can sure believe that.

When I reached the grandmother's house I took my time getting out and as soon as I knocked, the door opened as if she were looking out the window and saw me coming. My first impression of her was that she did not strike me as the sweet little cookie baker, rock all day and knit sweaters type of grandmother, because she was a five foot tall petite and little woman in her mid sixties, if I were to guess, with light little gray patches going through her brownish colored hair about, mid length to her shoulders, nice warm smile and soft voice, that made you feel right at home in her living room.

She said as she held her hand out to shake mine, "I am Margaret Snowden, but just call me Meg."

Even if we were close to the same age I didn't really feel comfortable with calling her by her first name, somehow it seemed disrespectful, but complied to her wishes just the same, but was hesitant. Her lovely home was neat as a pin and sparkling clean and so full of memories of past years. There were pictures all around on the dust-free tables, unlike mine, and I am so jealous, and if I were going to guess I would say some were of her parents, because of the very old frames that were from way back when. They had shadow backgrounds on them, like the ones my mom's family pictures had on them of my grandparents, and aunts and uncles. They were oval and the shadow behind them looked like dirty cloudy water, that had something to do with the lighting and were all taken in black and white.

"Would you like some coffee or tea or some other refreshment?" she asked, "and I also have some chocolate chip cookies I just baked."

"That sounds wonderful", I said. "I never turn down cookies, and coffee would be great." So she left the room and I kind of snooped a bit, but felt uneasy about meddling into her things too extensively. I mostly noticed all the hand-made crochet laying around in various places, all in different types of stitches and colors. There were so many antiques, figurines and lamps, and finely carved and polished cabinets and shelves with very old and beautiful and delicate china that was surely handed down from generation to generation and taken care of so tenderly, I would venture to guess. Most people would only dream of this type of home, not really live here, because it kind of reminded you of one of those old homes you would only find in a magazine, like the old Mississippi antebellum homes. I bet she did all her own housekeeping without any help, because I would never allow or trust a stranger with any of these beautiful antiques if I were her.

When Meg returned with the goodie's, I explained that I was trying to gather information on a case that started in the neighborhood where her granddaughter Regina lived and anything she could tell me would be greatly appreciated. When I mentioned Regina's name her eyes filled with tears and she just broke down, and I just had to go over and comfort her, but was a little surprised by the whole situation and felt so sorry for her, and I asked, "Meg, did I hurt your feelings or offend you in some way?"

She took out a white lace hanky which you don't see often, and dabbed her eyes very daintily, and said, "I am so sorry for being so silly, and no it is nothing you have done. It's just that I miss Ginny so, and her father refuses to let me see her or talk with her since she returned home after my daughter's death."

"But I thought she lived with you after her mother passed on?" I asked.

"She was only with me for a while, because her father was having a tough time accepting Millie's death, so he left Ginny with me and said it would be only temporarily, so I registered Ginny in school here for one semester and had her that summer and then he wanted her to come back home, before school started in the fall."

"But why does he not let Ginny visit you or you go to the house and see her?" I asked.

"I am not one to speak against others, but he is not and has never been a very nice man. I tried to talk Millie out of marrying him but you know how children are, and they will not listen to the parents, they have to make their own mistakes, and learn the hard way, which is exactly what happened to Millie. But, then it was too late, and after Ginny was born she thought she had no choice, but to stay with that man, such a waste on her part. I never saw any signs of physical abuse on her such as bumps or bruises but I know there was, and also mental and verbal abuse, but she would never complain to me in a million years for fear of having me say I told you so, which I never would, but I am sure he convinced her that no one would believe or listen to her on what was going on. He stopped letting her talk to me on the telephone or have any contact with me just before her death and I was so surprised when he asked me to take Ginny after Millie's death. He was so possessive of Millie and now I am afraid he is doing the same thing with Ginny and it just breaks my heart to think that he might be mentally abusing her. I have thought about going to the police about it but I have no proof and if he found out that I had reported him, I am afraid of what he might do to me or Ginny to get back at me, and trust me he would take action against one or both of us. So my hands are tied at this point, unless I can hire you to see if you can do something to help. Didn't you say you were a private investigator?" she asked.

I shook my head yes and said, "But I am already working on another case that is connected with you and Ginny and it would be a conflict of interest, but let me keep digging into this case and maybe the two will come together to where I can help both parties but I can't take any money from you at this point because it would not be entirely legal or ethical. But I have a gentleman that works with me sometimes and maybe he could pick up your end of the case. His name is Oscar and I will have him come back with me and we will talk to you together, and see if there is really any connection with the two cases. Will this be ok with you?" I asked Meg, and she said ok but to keep her informed of any changes and to tell Ginny she loves her, and if you see her I want to know that she is all right and well.

"Now another thing, Meg, how does Ginny's half brother Alton, come into the picture and what can you tell me about him?" and as I looked over at her she just sort of stiffened and started to move around in her seat very nervous-like.

"This one is bad news, and how did you hear about him? I hope he is not around my Ginny, Millie was deathly afraid of him, and he is a dangerous one, and should be locked up somewhere. Ernie had him with his first wife, Millie was his second wife, and it has never been said what had happened to the boy's mother. But I always got the feeling that there was something strange about her death. I don't know if Alton or Ernie or both had anything to do with her death but it wouldn't surprise me at all, since they are both violent and despicable people in my opinion but there has never been any proof to that effect. But Ernie always kept Alton away from Ginny and that always made me suspicious of him. I think the reason for Ernie taking Ginny from me was because he was afraid that she would talk to me about her home life and that he might have a few things to hide, but Ginny has never once said one thing against him or her brother, the poor thing is probably too scared to open her mouth about anything that goes on there. But I am sure that he does not let her too far from under his thumb to do anything outside their home except to go to school. I just have to know that she is all right, and Ernie was always very protective of her so maybe he will see that she is taken care of. But I still think in the old fashioned way that a young girl should have a woman in her life to watch over her and protect her and to talk to about just girl things when she feels like it, but he has taken that away from us. Please try and talk with her and assure her that I am always here for her, if she ever needs me." I could tell, as I was silently thinking to myself, that she was really hurting over all this, but the courts are most always on the side of the nearest living parent unless they are given some reason to doubt that person, and to think they are not taking care of the child. I sat with Meg a little longer and listened to her as she reminisced over her deceased daughter and her lost to her grand-daughter until I checked my watch to see that it was almost six in the evening, so I told her I would come back tomorrow with Oscar and let him talk to her about her case, and see if he could take on something else right now. She said ok, that it was nice to just talk to someone about these problems going on with Ginny and her father and just air things out into the open.

Chapter 17

That night when I got home it was getting late and I stopped at the store to pick up something to cook and when Ronnie came in I was just going over what I had learned from Meg and started to tell it all to him to get his opinion on the whole ordeal of things. Ronnie kind of leaned back in his easy chair and looked at me and said, "That is the saddest thing I have ever heard if it is all true."

"I believe it all," I said, "you would have to talk to this woman, she is so caring and good hearted and devoted to Ginny completely if her father would allow it. And this child seemed so withdrawn and sad with no one to talk to but this angry old man, and it just does not seem fair. I am an outsider so I can't help her but I will surely try and find out what is going on there and maybe she can be with her grandmother at least part of the time. But you know, I wonder if any of this has something to do with Robert, because the way Meg talked the brother and dad were very capable of any kind of violence, so I guess I need to get down and dirty and check very deep into their background."

Ronnie just frowned at me and put his arm around me and had a worried look on his face and said "Please be careful and don't take any unnecessary chances and call Arnie and tell him what you have learned and keep him informed of your whereabouts most all of the time when you are going out, ok?"

I nodded yes and said, "You worry too much, you can't get rid of me that easy. But I am going to call Oscar right now and have him tag along with me for the next few days just to make you happy."

He said, "That will work, so make the call now, please."

"Oh you are such a nagger," I said, "Nag,nag,nag" but I knew down deep that he was right as usual, which made my temper flare a little, but just a little.

"Suzy, I plan on the two of us growing old together and I couldn't think of anything happening to you", he said.

And I said, "What do you mean growing old together babe, we are already there."

He said, "Then let me rephrase it, growing older together, I'm not ready to throw in the towel yet, toots." and he popped me on the backside with a big grin. I got a hold of Oscar at Lillian's and told him about my day and all that I had found out and asked him to stick to me like glue for a few days and to go talk to Meg with me tomorrow, and he said he would try and work me in, and then he let out a big old ugly laugh, which I had to smile to myself.

Ronnie was not ready for bed yet, so we discussed the case further, and came up with some scenarios that made pretty good sense, but kind of out in left field if you let your imagination run away with you, so we stopped imagining the worse and got back to the more sensible things, that maybe Regina got into some kind of trouble, and the dad found out and wanted revenge on anyone that happened to be close at hand at the time but just too many maybes and what ifs, but I needed more proof, that's always the one thing you have to think about, all the pieces have to fit together. I think I need to go back to the neighborhood where all this started and nose around a little more, and while deep in thought the phone rang, startling Ronnie and I, and we both jumped, boy are we jittery, but with good reason. I answered it and it was Arnie, "Suzy", he asked, "wasn't one of the guys you were questioning named George Morrison?"

"Yeah", I said, "what's up, I was just thinking of going out there tomorrow and talking to him and his wife."

"Well you won't talk to this guy, because he's dead, I am out at his house now investigating his murder, or at least that's what we are calling it so far. Someone shot him in the back of the head, and his wife just found him. She and their daughter were out for the evening and we don't have a time of death as of yet but the body is still semi warm, so it hasn't been too long. If you would like to come out here it will be all right, but just don't get in the way, and don't come alone. Have Ronnie come with you or wait until tomorrow morning and I will brief you on the details. It's your choice, kid."

"No, I think I will come over now", I said, "before the trail, if there is one, gets too cold, but I would like to call Oscar and have him come here now, since he is just next door from you, if that's ok."

"Yea, that's cool, but don't tell me why Oscar is in the area, because I really don't care to know. I am sure there is an interesting story there, but that's ok, I don't think I am ready for it quite yet. Just be very careful, I don't know if there is any connection to your case, but you never can tell."

When we hung up I explained the conversation to Ronnie and he just sort of scrooched up his face and let out a long sigh, but wouldn't hear of me leaving the house this late without him, so I humored him by saying it was ok for him to tag along, fat chance I'd ever get out without him.

When we drove up at the Morrison's, the wife and daughter were out in one of the six or eight patrol cars that were out front and to my surprise Lillian was there with them, which was probably a pretty good idea. Oscar was inside already and as close to the body as they would let him get, and snooping around for some evidence of any kind, but the officers had been pretty thorough and were not giving us much on their take of what had happened. Then the news people from all over had started swarming like a bunch of flies on manure, but the officers were very closed-mouthed about the whole murder thing, imagine that, which had not officially been ruled as that yet. When Arnie spotted me he came over and filled me in some, and seemed confused of what might be happening in the neighborhood, with Robert missing and now this a year later, something is beginning to smell about this whole thing, but still no connection yet to the two. Arnie announced that his guys were going to start a door to door search and questioning, and an investigation of all the residents on the next two blocks, which are long country blocks, to see if any one heard or saw anything suspicious.

"Maybe something will turn up", he said, "I would also like to talk to Oscar and his lady friend over there."

I explained that she was the one that hired me to investigate her son's disappearance. Arnie said, "That's got to be rough on her, and now this going on right in her neighborhood."

I walked over to Mrs. Morrison and she looked like she was almost completely wrung out and I suggested she stay somewhere else for the night, when the police were finished with her. Lillian then stepped in and offered them a place, for as long as they needed it, and she accepted without hesitation. Now I think Oscar has found him a jewel of a lady, and I thought to myself, you sure better hang on to her, old boy, for they are very rare these days, and I will have to be sure and tell him that. I don't think I will get much out of the wife tonight, so that will have to wait until tomorrow. I went back in to see the body before it was taken away and the room was in a mess, like someone was looking for something, and I remembered about the letter Oscar had found the day we were looking around but, there may not be any connection there. Maybe Oscar will remember what the name was of the place that had sent it and what type of place it was, I have slept since then, so I can't remember much about it, but he has a photographic memory.

"Looks like there was a drink in a glass on the table next to the couch and an ash tray with a cigarette butt, but maybe it's his, and just one glass, so it most likely was his. There was a stack of magazines on the couch with some thrown on the floor, and everything from the desk is all on the floor. I wonder if the killer found what he was looking for. I don't see much more to get into here, so I may as well wrap it up and go over to Lillian's and see if the wife said anything to her and have her keep her ears open wide and try to pick up on anything that might tell us more about what is going on here."

Lillian went in and fixed up Robert's room for Joan and Joanie to occupy until they could go back home, and will probably be a good while until it is in any shape to accommodate them again. It is going to be very hard for them to stay in that house, after George was killed there and not knowing if it will even be safe for a while, which I'm sure the killer is long gone, but there's is no way of knowing if he found what he was after. Lillian made us all some coffee and they put Joanie to bed while the adults all sat around discussing what had just happened, and Joan became upset all over again, which, I guess we were very insensitive to her feelings, and so she excused herself to go to bed. Oscar and Ronnie were talking about the mess the house was in and wondering what the killer was hunting for, and that's when I broke in and asked him about the letter he found on the desk the day we were there.

"Oh yeah", he said, "I remember, it was from Drake's Concrete company, something about a delivery they had made but didn't give any information about who it was delivered to. Only that the records were misplaced and they would send the paperwork on it when they found them. Maybe Joan can help us with that in the morning before she goes down to the police station."

"Well, let's call it a night", Ronnie said. And we all agreed. I could barely keep my eyes open any longer.

Chapter 18

The next morning was Saturday, but no rest for me. I got up and Ronnie made coffee for me and was already outside picking up limbs and burning them and doing some other things around there, already had the oil changed in the vehicles and then came into the bedroom and woke me up to go for our morning walk but before we could get out the door, my darling daughter called to tell me about her new gentleman friend and that took about ten minutes and I listened while Ronnie was frowning, and standing at the door impatiently, waiting for me to hang up. When Annie and I start talking it turns into a long mother daughter gab session and he usually just lets us go until we are finished. Annie and I don't get to see each other very often and she only lives about an hour away and she and I travel in different worlds but we do try to get together with all the rest of the family when we can. I told her a little about what I was working on, but that is not her cup of tea, and she could care less about my work, and hers is very boring to me, but we try to put up with each other. I am very proud of both of my kids, they have never been in any trouble and have always had a decent job and worked so hard, and always given their job a hundred percent of themselves.

After our walk I got a shower and got dressed and went over to talk to Joan but I had to wait until she got back from the police station, so I went outside and took a short walk around the neighborhood to see if anyone was out, since this was, after all, Saturday and most people venture out and work some around the house but boy was I wrong. I walked down the road towards

Regina's house and the place looked deserted, so I thought I would just nose around a bit but there were not any cars in the yard or driveway and I wasn't sure that I should go it alone since the murder last night, but I talked myself into doing it anyway, so I just slipped around the back and took a peek at the back yard, what there was of it. Gee whiz, these people have a thing about swimming pools, and this one even has a hot tub not far from the pool, must be nice, and the pools are in the ground, which yea, I have one too but it is an above the ground like all the red necks out there. Annie says mine looks like a giant condom. She can be ugly sometimes, but what a way with words she has. Something hit me strange about this pool, but I couldn't figure for the life of me what it was or exactly put my finger on it, but maybe it would come to me later. There was a lot of wooded land in the back of the house and I just wondered how many acres there were and just how far it went back into those woods. It was kind of creepy, like someone was back there, and watching me as I snooped. The back of the house had a nice wide deck going to the pool, but not all around it, and a gazebo that was pretty good size and painted white and a walkway leading up to the house, with plants on both sides. Boy what a nice set up, looks like someone spent a lot of money. There was a patio table and bench and chairs that looked fairly new but could have been freshly painted also. Why would any child be unhappy with all these luxuries for her alone, but maybe there is another explanation for Regina's moods. Oh well, who knows what keeps teenagers happy these days especially young girls. Boy I never knew how to keep mine happy all the time. It was just a hit and miss deal.

I walked slowly back to Lillian's, still having the odd feeling that I was being watched, to see if Joan had returned and she was just driving up, so I we went in to see if she could tell me anything else on the murder last night.

"Joan", I said, "you know that someone had tossed your house upside down, so to speak, and do you have any idea what they were looking for?"

"No, I really don't have any idea", she said, "but I am afraid they will come back if they didn't find what they were looking for."

"The last time Oscar and I talked to you we saw a letter on the desk from Drakes Concrete Company, do you know what happened to it? It could be important in finding who did this to George." I said. But she just sat there and looked confused about what I was talking about, so I had to explain further.

Joan asked what did her mail have to do with George's death, and I said, "Maybe nothing, but we have to follow all the leads, or what looks like leads or the evidence. So could we please go over after a while and see if we can find the letter, and is there a special place that George might put something to keep it safe?"

She said that there was a couple of places that he could hide something he didn't want her to know about and that she had watched him hide things before, when he didn't know she was watching. I said that it was worth a try.

"Has there been anyone suspicious hanging around or any visitors lately that you have seen?" I asked.

"Not really, just Ernie Carson about three days ago and that he and George were arguing about something, but when I asked about it, he just shrugged and told me to go back inside and not worry about it. But you know, it was a bit weird that Ernie was even at our house", she said, "because he has never associated with us much since his wife died. But George didn't tell me what was going on and Joanie called me to come and do something for her. Do you think the police think I had anything to do with hurting George?" Joan asked.

"They always check out the spouse first in every case where there is murder involved", I said, "but with your alibi and people seeing you and Joanie out, I don't think you have anything to worry about at this point.

"I have to make arrangements for his funeral today or tomorrow and Joanie is terribly upset that her dad is not ever coming back home. After all he was a good dad to her and was so good and patient with her. They were the best of friends, and he and I had our ups and downs, like all other couples, but nothing serious. I don't know of any enemies he had that would go to this extreme, so there must have been something going on that I didn't catch on to. I do miss him already, and do not know what I will do next. I think we are alright financially for now, until I can get a job, but the emotional strain is greater than the financial one. I am not really thinking clearly yet, so I have to just take it one day at a time, and get through the funeral and all."

"What can you tell me about Ernie's son Alton", I asked, "and did you know him very well?"

"I don't know a lot about him except that he has not been allowed to come around their house since Ernie's wife died, and boy is he a real piece of work. I think, from what I saw of him he could be a violent person easily, and never blink an eye. He seemed to not have much of a conscience, which to me would be a very dangerous trait. George wouldn't let him anywhere near Joanie, for some reason, but I was glad he felt that way, and that's about all I can tell you about him. Now Ernie on the other hand did not seem as cold feeling, but I didn't exactly feel all warm and fuzzy when he was around either." Joan said, "I am really getting tired after the third degree the police gave me and now with you, but I know you are just trying to help and so are they."

"Well, maybe I can talk to you later and hopefully you can remember more. One more thing, did you touch anything in the room when you found George except the phone or move any of the items in the room, because something was out of place besides the things strewn around the room. Seems something was missing from the front room since the day I was there last. Can you tell what it might be, or can we check one more time to see if you can tell. Do you feel like going over there with me today, or would you like to wait until Monday, when I return to ask more questions?"

"We can take a quick look now, if you think it might help." she said, "Besides I have to go in there eventually, so I just as well do it now and get it over with."

"Ok then", I said hesitantly, "let's do it."

When we walked into the front door of Joan's house it had already gotten an odor working and it was pretty strong, so she opened a window and put a fan on, but it wasn't much help. I was not going to stay very long, so I would just suck it up and go on. Joan pointed to a table that once had a large statue of a Dutch girl on it, and put her hand over her mouth and gasped, and said that the statue was missing, who would want that, it was a gift from Millie Carson, Ernie's wife, now that is a strange turn of events.

"You have a real good eye", she said, "if you spotted that last night before I did, I live here and all." She looked around some more to just eyeball everything to see if she could see anything else missing, but with no luck, so we decided to go our separate ways for now, and let things set another day, so our minds would clear for another look around some other time.

I called Arnie and told him about going for a walk around the neighborhood and what I did or didn't see, about having a feeling that someone was watching me at the Carson's, and about the statue missing from Joan's house.

Arnie said, "You are taking too many chances nosing around there alone, and I think it's just plain nuts, and careless", he pointed out rather harshly, "so please be careful."

I asked him to meet me at the office later when I could get back in, that I wanted to go over the things I had uncovered about the Carson's, which was not much, but maybe a few things that didn't really jive. I think I will take my car and drive next door to the Carson's and try to talk to Ernie, looks like they may be there now.

When I knocked, Regina came to the door rather quickly and was not too friendly, or maybe just a little afraid to say much, but did invite me to come in and just as I stepped in Ernie came right behind her and wanted to know why I was there. I thought to myself that was very blunt but tried to not let him see my surprise at his very rude attitude.

"I need to ask you some questions about the murder last night." I said and he looked a little taken off guard, but just the same, tried to answer calmly.

He said, "We were not home until late." and about that time Regina just looked up at him and kind of had a blank but kind of a wondering look on her face, which told me he could possibly be lying, boy am I suspicious of people but in this business you get that way. He asked who had been murdered, but didn't act a bit taken by the death of George Morrison, when I told him. Regina sort of took it all in but didn't add anything to the conversation but I think she was hiding something or afraid to say anything in front of her father, so I'll just let it go for now and talk to her when I could catch her alone. I still needed to tell her the message her grandmother had sent her but not while Ernie was around.

I left and headed home for the rest of my Saturday and to get some things done around the house. As I walked in Mandy drove right in behind me and asked if we were going to church tomorrow, and invited us to stay for the luncheon they were having for the new pastor, after church. Personally I liked the old one better, but didn't really have a choice in the matter and I had to decline on the invitation, because Ronnie doesn't like all the gatherings of all those people, nothing personal against them, but he is a little shy when he gets in a crowd, so we usually don't stay. Also Mandy couldn't find her spare keys for her car and wanted me to come over and help her look for them, so we searched everywhere, but with no luck, and I told her that when her housekeeper came Monday they would show up. When I got back home the weather was beginning to look dreary and cold so I just huddled up with a blanket in my easy chair and I guess I fell asleep, because I was startled by a noise I guess was the phone and managed to wake up enough to hear someone whisper something that sounded like a threat, and ordered me to butt out of their business and quit nosing around where I had not been invited or I would be very sorry. My face kind of went hot and I shivered a little and it kind of scared me at first, but then I tried to get a grip, enough to see if I recognized the whisper on the other end, but I don't think I had ever heard that voice before but then a whisper is hard to distinguish clear. But it was definitely a male voice that was trying to give me a serious warning but I don't alarm that easy, after I was in a deep sleep, and I just started yelling into the phone back at the jerk, and asking who is this, but they began to laugh and hung up. The first thing I thought was what a whack job this was, with a very warped since of humor, if that is what it was. Sick, sick, I thought to myself.

Ronnie came in from the back yard and I guess I had a real strange look on my face, because he wanted to know what was wrong, so I explained about the phone call.

"The thing about it", I said, "is that I never have been bothered with anyone following me or any threats until I started digging again on this case, and I have been so careful at keeping track of the people I have talked to, and in what order, and I haven't had any problem until I talked to the Carsons, seems that these people just keep popping up. I need to know what happened to Ernie's first wife and what she died of, if it was a disease, accident, or something else. I will have the death certificate pulled from the courthouse records and find out what the cause of death was. Well the only thing with that is if she died in another county then no records will be at this courthouse and that may present a small problem. Oh well, we will see. I bet it's a safe bet to say that she didn't die from natural causes."

I looked at my notes closely and listed all the suspects I had on George's death, but I couldn't prove anything at this time, but that would surely change in the near future, I'd bet. I called Oscar and told him about the weird phone call and asked what he thought about it and what he thought of meeting me here Monday morning, and that way someone would be here after Ronnie left for work, I am just a big chicken is all there is to it, but he thought that was the smart thing to do at this point. So he will be my shadow all that day so I can get some work done without looking over my shoulder.

Chapter 19

Sunday morning after church we had Oscar and Lillian over for an afternoon lunch and kind of discussed things and everyone gave input about who or what was all involved in the last few days' developments.

"It looks like some of the pieces are beginning to go together", I said, "but we were still a long ways from all the answers to this puzzle."

Lillian asked just what I had been thinking about the last few days, did I think that George's death had anything to do with Robert's disappearance and I shook my head, that I was not sure but it was very possible. I was trying to be as gentle about it as possible but I am not a gentle person. Everyone tells me how insensitive I can be, especially Ladonna in her sweet snotty way, imagine that.

Lillian kind of looked down and got a real sad look about her and tears came to her eyes and Oscar reminded her that she knew there was a big chance that Robert would not return to her, but she said, "I just kept hoping against hope that he might still be alive, but isn't it still too early to tell if any thing has happened to him?" she asked.

"I wish I could give you some assurance that he was going to be found ok, Lillian", I said, "but it has just been too long and just no trace of him at all."

"Well", she said, "I guess I will just have to accept whatever happens and try to move on." and she squeezed Oscars hand and looked at him and said, "At least it's not like it was, I have someone to share good or bad news with, whichever it happens to be." Oscar kind of grinned back at her and I could tell they were going to be a couple for a long time, yep, he is hooked all right. It has come none too soon. Without being too mushy about it, he really is a pretty good Joe. I managed to get Oscar off to the side and ask him if he had found out who Lillian was talking to pretty heatedly the other day and he said she told him that it was a co-worker that seems to have an eye on her and is pretty persistent about wanting to go out with her and she told him finally at work that she was involved with someone. So hopefully he will leave her alone, or he will have to persuade him a little. I just shook my fist at him.

The next morning the air had a chill in it that just would not quit, so I drug out the sweaters and jeans and a warm jacket and sat at the kitchen table and had coffee to warm my old bones, but it seems to take longer to move very fast in the mornings these days, so I just sat a while and read the morning paper and waited for Oscar to get here. About that time someone knocked on the door and I looked out and saw his old beater out front. He came in just a shivering and complaining about the cold and hunting the coffee.

"How is Lillian this morning", I asked, "did she get to feeling better about things after you two left?"

"Yeah, she wants Robert to show up is all, and you and I both know there is not much of a chance of that, and I think down deep, she does too, and that he is probably going to turn up dead. Suze, she is an amazing woman and I hate to see her hurting like this, but what else can we do to try to give her some closure to it all?" He looked very helpless, like Ronnie looks at me sometime when he knows there is nothing he can do about some situations, such as Jonathon living without his mom near, but you just have to roll with the flow until something happens. Oscar is mature enough to realize this, but doesn't like it just the same, and that is what love is all about.

I said, “You want to take care of each other no matter what.” but he is such a macho person he just said, “Yeah, yeah.” and went for another cup of coffee.

He just shook his head and said, “Why do you women always have to be so ga ga about everything, you always have a silly answer for everything, I guess it is just a chick thing, huh? Let's go.” he said abruptly and was out the door before I could answer, which was the whole idea of it, I'm sure.

Oscar was kind of slumped in the front seat dozing, I suppose, when I happened to look up and see the same old clunker of a pickup following me again, looked like the same blue one from before, and I tried to get Oscars attention, but with no luck at first, then I turned on the rock music loud and scared him awake, and told him to stay down, but to look out the side mirror and that was the same truck I had seen before.

Oscar said, “Suze pull into the station ahead and see if he pulls in or hangs back and if I can I will sneak out the door and get around back of him and jump him.” but when I slowed down he zoomed around me and I guess he got a look and saw someone in the car with me.

"You think he saw me, Suze?"

I said, "I'm not sure, it happened so fast, but something sure scared him off, not so brave now, as he was when he thought it was a woman alone, but he doesn't know me very well does he?"

"Boy that's an understatement", he said, "a woman with a gun, that's about as nasty as you can get."

"Well it's started again, and it makes me madder than an old wet hen that this guy thinks he can scare me off, I want another crack at him, and I'm sure I will get it pretty soon. We are getting too close for comfort but I won't quit now. How about lunch, I will buy, but after we stop at the courthouse and check for a death certificate on Ernie Carson's first wife."

"Yeah, what did you have in mind?"

"How about Malone's Bar and Grill?" I asked.

"Sounds good." he answered but when we got to the courthouse there was no death certificate for the first wife, and that was what I was afraid of, which meant she had lived somewhere else at the time of her death. Well that's a different turn of events. But anything is possible.

So we headed out and as we started in to Malone's for a sandwich and cold beer, I turned to walk in and caught a glimpse out of the corner of my eye of a familiar face. Oscar was watching me closely and asked, "What is it kid, see something you don't like?"

"Yeah, I don't like it, ok", but I said, "Who is the dame with him, oh boy, let me get my camera."

"Suzy, what the hell are you doing?"

"You'll see, see that pig over there, he is the one that gave me the black eye, and it's payback time now, but you gotta swear that you won't rat me out to Ronnie."

"Now I'm not good at lying to friends, and you know that he and I are buds." he said.

"I'm not asking you to lie, just don't tell him."

As I got behind my car I grabbed the camera and began snapping one picture after another thinking how I was going to get these to his wife or significant other or whatever she was. I wonder if this is the same woman that picked him up at the jail the other night, I'm betting it's not because she looks like a working girl, and I don't mean like a secretary or better known these day's as an administrative assistant, but just in case I'll have a picture, and it's said they are worth a thousand words.

"You sure are an evil woman, Suzy", he said, "this

sure is mean and hateful even for you."

"Well you know what they say a woman scorned and all that."

"Yeah, but you just have to get your revenge, don't you?"

"Yeah, well that sore eye he gave me is going to take a lot of revenge on my part, and this is only the start of it." Oscar just shook his head and mumbled something obscene under his breath. After we had lunch we drove across town and I slipped the pictures under the guys door, now get yourself out of this one buddy. Surprisingly enough I didn't get as much satisfaction as I thought I would from messing the guy up, but I still think he deserved it and maybe I'll let it go at that, and then again, maybe not.

When I pulled away from the curb, I caught a look at the old blue pickup coming straight for us, and Oscar pulled out his gun and fired, once into his windshield, and just then I heard a shot gun blast explode into mine, and I thought, it has to be two of them, because the shot came from the passenger side of the truck, and he kind of wobbled to the side of the road like maybe the driver was hit or stunned, and then he sped off with us right behind him, with only half a windshield, going down I-10 intersecting into loop 610. As traffic was starting to crowd in we lost them with no clue as to where they had gone. I turned and asked Oscar what he thought of this turn of things, and he said, “We need to stop and call the cops and let them know about this incident. Suzy, did you see any numbers on the plates?"

"No," I said, "they were shaded over with something, but it had to be two of them, to shoot that straight and accurate."

"Boy they made hash of your car, and how are you going to explain that one to Ronnie?" he asked.

"Very cautiously", I said "I will handle it, hopefully, but hope it can be fixed, but since it has been in the shop twice, already this year, no bets."

After we tried to talk to the police officers with full cooperation on our part, it was a no win situation, because, all we kept hearing from them was you must have pissed off someone and they are retaliating against you, Mrs. Lighter. Why do cops always treat women like they are brainless? I knew the real reason behind all the shooting at us, so I said that I guess I'd have to handle it myself, but the police said I had a big imagination.

"Yeah maybe", I told one of them, "but when we crack open a missing person and murder case for you, don't try to take the credit with the public on the six o'clock news. I don't want to see a lot of patting on the back and tooting your own horn crap either." I said and then I walked off snubbing my nose at them, "So much for helping the peacemakers around here." I grumbled. As I walked away I mumbled a few choice words under my breath and Oscar grabbed me by the arm and told me to get in the car before I get us both thrown in jail.

"Boy what a weenie." I said.

Oscar began to shake his finger at me and yelling at me to can it, but I hate cops sometimes and I wanted them to know.

I drove my car straight back to the house so we could pick up Oscar's truck, since my car was in no shape to drive, especially without a front windshield on this cold wintery day. Oscar would not let me leave the house without him by my side and I guess I was grateful for that, but I couldn't even imagine in my wildest dreams of having a body guard every minute of the day, but when Ronnie sees my car he won't let me out of the house at all. It could be worse, I could have had to depend on my sister to chauffeur me around. Oh no, not in this lifetime.

Chapter 20

When Ronnie came home and took one look at my car, he raised the roof, as to say, my ears will burn for the next six months but he soon got over it and called the repair shop to see how long it would take to fix it. The guys there would not commit to any time frame, until Ronnie threatened to call the shop down the street and that was all it took. The greedy buggers, the guy finally said it would be ready in a couple of days if he could get a windshield in town and not have to order it. Guess you will have to drive the backup truck he said for a few days or get Oscar to drive you around, which I would prefer that to you taking things into your hands, which we both knew where that might lead to. So I agreed to call Oscar and have him pick me up .in the morning and run around with me, but just for one day, I said, and he agreed reluctantly.

The next morning Oscar and I went downtown to the police station to see if there was any news on the two men from yesterday that were shooting at us, and the officer in charge said that there was a witness that drove by about the time the truck was speeding down the freeway and he said that one guy looked at him from an older blue truck, he gave a description of the man driving and that he was between the age of twenty five and thirty five. White, medium build, but couldn't tell exactly how tall he was, because he was sitting down and he went by pretty fast. The officer wanted us to look through some books of mug shots or better known as photo's of ex-convicts to see if we recognized anyone there, so just by chance I started with the letter C's to see if I could check and see if Alton Carson's picture was in there, but if they were not originally from this city or state it would not be here but it’s worth a try.

Bingo, there he is, bigger than life, but he didn't look familiar to me. Oscar looked real hard and said, "That could have been the driver of the truck, but I can't be sure enough to convict him yet. I didn't get a direct look at him, so we will have to pursue it further and get a personal and up close look at him next time, and I'm dead sure there will be a next time, if you will pardon the expression. Suze, I don't want you to leave the house without someone with you, just take a look at this rap sheet and tell me he is not dangerous. He was convicted of murder, but got off on a loophole where the lawyer lost evidence conveniently, smells like a payoff, and the jury couldn't honestly convict him with a clear conscience, so they had to let him go, but he was in and out of trouble as a child and spent most of his young years in some sort of hospital or juvenile detention.

"Let's get the doctor's name that took care of him as a child", I said, "and see if he can shed some light on things. If he was unusually difficult, and I suspect he was, the doctors will remember him, and that will give us something more to go on, instead of trying to put it all together ourselves."

"I am afraid we have a real bad one on our hands, Suzy", Oscar said, "and let's don’t underestimate him, or his abilities to take the law into his own hands, and if he has help, which it looks that way, then we are looking for two possible killers capable of most anything. We looked further into the C’s and there was Ernie there also, or better known as Ernest Alton Carson, which all of their records were old stuff, but I'll bet Alton hasn't been out very long. Now Ernest on the other hand was a different story, he had stayed pretty clean for almost twenty years and Regina is probably the reason so he could give her a good home and at least has one good child to be proud of, Lord knows Alton was no prize according to all his past history.

"I am still curious about Regina's mother Millie and the cause of death, but unless anyone can give us something on it we will probably never know." I said.

"Was Alton the only child Ernie and his first wife ever had?" Oscar asked.

"I didn't find any birth record of any other children, but that doesn't really mean there was not another one born." I said. "I will do a bit more checking on it, but I wouldn't hold my breath. As we both know weird things can happen easily with this family, I have found."

"Oscar", I said, "I will go see the doctor that took care of Alton when he was younger and you go and interview the..."

"Whoa; stop!" Oscar said and held up his hand in my face, "I am not leaving you at all and besides Ronnie would have my head in the palm of his hand. Remember you have a shadow until this mess is over and done with, so get used to it, and let's go to see the doctor together. Besides I will push a little harder than you, even though you are more intimidating with your grandmother pushy attitude, but together we can probably get further with him and hopefully, he is not too old to remember Alton, because you have to remember, that was a long time ago."

"No", I said, "from all the trouble he caused his family, I'll bet the doctor or someone in that office will know something that will help us. But we will see later on when we get to Austin, Alabama."

"What", Oscar exclaimed, "they are from Alabama?"

"Yeah, I guess I forgot to mention that, but we can fly a lot faster than we can drive it."

Oscar kind of frowned and said, "Yeah, you did fail

to mention that and you know I don't like to fly, besides when you said that, I thought you were talking Texas hill country and all that, but you are not going alone, so I will have to make an exception this time."

"Ok", I said, "we will go by and get your clothes and then we will go and get mine, and head for the airport. Boy, Ronnie is not going to be happy about this trip, Oscar, so you had better come in with me and catch my back."

"Oh no, I'm staying in the truck where I belong, so hurry up."

Ronnie just pouted about a minute and said he wished he could go with us but that he was glad Oscar was going and to still be very careful and that he loved me and said he would put the light on for me for whenever I returned, boy that was easy, hmm, he will probably retaliate when I get back. But he knows I have to do whatever it takes to solve a case, so he is always understanding when it comes to a case.

When we were settled on the plane, Oscar said, "You know, the doctor as I said is pretty old, so you can bet that a lot of his patients are too, and have been coming a long time to see him, so they probably knew Alton and his mother and you know how those old grandmas and grandpas love to gossip about other people especially from way back from the past, and it's worth a try."

I just stared at him with fire in my eyes as he said grandmas and grandpas, and he just rolled his eyes up at me and grinned but even though I knew he was right, I was not going to admit it, not in this lifetime anyway and give him the satisfaction. Sometime he gets on my last nerve, but I have to admit he was fun to have around, of course I would never share that with him. It would go right to his head and I would never be able to stand him at all. Oscar and I pulled up to the doctor's office and went different ways, as I walked up to the doctor I knew instantly that he was the one I was looking for, because he looked just like Santa with the beard and pot belly included and I asked him if he had been there in the same building for a long time, and he answered with, "Practically all my life and was born here in town not a mile from my office, and still live on our old home place that my father bought many years ago.

"What can I do for you?" he asked.

"I'm checking on one of your patients from a long time ago, Alton Carson."

"Now let me see", he said as he scratched his chin, "Alton Carson, oh yeah." then he looked a little frightened and would not look straight at me. "You know I can't say a lot, because of doctor patient confidentiality and that was a long time ago, but why do you want to know?" he asked.

"We want to know if there was anything unusual about him, like violent or unruly or just anything that might make his behavior stand out as different from other children."

"Well", he said, "since Sara is deceased, I guess it would be ok to tell you that he was a very different boy, but Sara always was so protective of him and always tried to protect him from any talk or any action against him for the evil things he would do. You see Sara was from a very wealthy family and Alton was given everything a child would want and if he was in any trouble he was protected by his mother's money and was always bought out of any trouble he got into. I never knew what happened to Ernie and him, they just moved away after Sara's death and seemed to drop off the face of the earth."

"After Sara's death?" I asked. "Was there anything

suspicious about her death, doctor?"

"I don't know, but the doctor that took care of her and examined her body after her death mysteriously disappeared and was never found."

"What was the doctor's name?" I asked.

"Doctor Dan Ramey, from Jenkins, the next town over from us, but he had no relatives that anyone could find so there was no one to really complain about the disappearance and the local police couldn't solve that case and it's still listed as an unsolved disappearance case. From what I hear he was pretty much a loner and the only doctor in town and I think his nurse reported him missing."

"Why didn't she let you treat her?" I asked.

"Because Ernie convinced her that he was a much better doctor than I and much more experienced, so they traveled over there to him, and it seemed very mysterious to me, but that was Sara's wishes, so Ernie went along with it. But I do remember that I had heard that she was cremated, so there was no body to examine after her death."

"What were her symptoms?" I asked.

He sort of shrugged and said that Ernie would not let him get close enough to her to find out.

"So, there could have been foul play, and possible injuries for all anyone knows?" I asked. And he shook his head yes reluctantly. "Doctor you said that Alton had done a lot of evil things, can you tell me any of them without breaking a confidence, like maybe gossip or just hear-say that you trusted to be truth?"

"Well, I do know that Sara had a little girl before Alton was born and that she supposedly fell down the stairs and was killed instantly when she was seven and Alton was only five. Sara said that it was an accident and no one suspected anything was wrong with the statement until the house was set on fire and the family dog and puppies were lost in the fire, but the fire department couldn't say if it was set deliberately or an accident or either they were paid off and suddenly, they did come up with two brand new fire trucks, so everyone was a little suspicious, but no one had the nerve to go against Sara or her family. Then there were kids in the neighborhood that were scared to death and wouldn't play with Alton and kept their animals locked up when he was home and not away at private school or hospitals or correctional schools."

"Ok, doc", I said, "I get the picture ok, say no more, he was just an all around bad seed is what you are saying huh?"

"That's the way I always saw it and most of the others around here had the same opinion."

"One more thing, doc? Was there another old home place here that Sara and Ernie had?"

"Why yes there is, by the way and someone still keeps it up in tip top shape, over on Hayes road, about five miles out, has an old barn and home place and about fifty acres of land with it, if you'd like I could show you how to get there or at least direct you there, but I wouldn't go out there alone."

"No," I said, "I have my partner here with me and we will take a ride out there, and thanks very much, you have been very helpful."

"If I may ask," he said, "what exactly is going on, the last I heard about Alton he had gone away to prison for a long time, I take it he is out now and causing trouble elsewhere, is that correct?"

"You are absolutely right doc, but I don't think you have anything to worry about."

"Maybe not", he said, "but if you are after him you should be very careful, that's a real mean one." and just shook his head and looked a little frightened again.

"Yeah doc, I have seen some of his handiwork first hand and I will take every precaution that I possibly can. Thanks again."

When I came out Oscar was talking to an old woman that looked like she had one foot in the grave, but was still talking a mile a minute, so age had not affected her gossiping in the least. When he looked my way he could tell I had scored in the info department so he broke loose and came over to me. I was grinning and he obviously picked up on that because he said, "You look like the cat that ate the canary, so what gives?"

"Well, let's take a ride and we will talk on the way. Did you get anything we can use from some of the other patients, by the way, or just visiting with the town's people?" I asked.

"Yeah, but let's compare notes on the way out, you know we still have to make that flight this evening, back to Houston and I told Lillian I would be back by eight and take her out dancing."

"I know, I told Ronnie I would try to be back early enough to spend some time with him and maybe go over to Ronnie Jr's to have a campfire outside with him and the kids, so we can play redneck with them or at least seem like we fit in, but Ronnie Jr. always says we can keep our shoes on if it makes us feel better so we don't feel so much like back woods folks. Didn't know I raised such an abrupt and sarcastic kid. But I guess I deserve whatever he pops back at me, since I give him a hard time about living further out than I do in the woods."

Chapter 21

When we started out to Sara and Ernie's old home place, Oscar filled me in about what he had learned from people that remembered Sara and Ernie and especially Alton, which he picked up on as the evil one, and the stories were about the same as the doctors, only a little more explicit. He was a terribly angry child and some of the neighbors that knew him well were frightened into staying away from the whole family and also described him as a bad one from the word go. Oscar and I agreed that he was a lot more dangerous than we thought so this took a lot more thinking on our part about what to do next, but we both felt sure that the two missing boys were surely dead and as soon as we get back home we would notify the local authorities of what information we had uncovered and let them handle it but I just couldn't walk away without answers for Lillian, we both did agree on that one thing. As we drove up to the old house, there didn't appear to be any one around, so I got out of the car and started to nose around. Oscar went around to an old barn and waved me over and lo and behold as I walked in there, it was bigger than life, the old beat up blue pickup truck and now pretty well damaged from our bullet holes. This is the reason I couldn't find it anywhere, he had driven it out of state.

I looked up just in time to see Oscar starting to back out of the barn slowly, and it looked like he had just stumbled onto a hornet's nest, and he motioned to me to do the same, and he turned and said, "Let’s get the hell out of here now before someone sees us and warns Alton or Ernie that we were here." So we both nearly ran to the rent car and headed to the airport without delaying for even a second.

On the plane Oscar turned and said, "I am going by the house after we get the truck and pick Lillian up and we are all going to stay at your house tonight." and I started to raise my hand and he shook his head as he interrupted me before I had a chance to say a word, "I know you are supposed to go to Ronnie Jr's tonight, so we will all go and play redneck for the night with you. I don't want us to split up for a moment with this maniac on the loose, ok?" he asked.

"Yeah, you are probably right and I'll call Ronnie and tell him to be on his guard and be sure everything is locked up tight. You know if anyone saw us at Alton's house in Alabama they will report it immediately to him, so I want us to be ready for him, police and all, so call Arnie as soon as you get home."

"Ok, but do you think we should go around my family and won't that put them in danger?"

"No, he just wants you and me or I wouldn't suggest we go over there." he said. "But we don't want him to think that we are changing anything in our lives especially for him, he would love that, thinking he is scaring us. But we can warn Ronnie Jr. to lock up tighter than a drum and keep his pistol next to the bed, so he can be ready for anything that might develop. He is as good a shot as I am. This guy is crazy and doesn't care who knows it apparently, and I will feel safer if we are close to Ronnie Jr. and family, but as I said, Suzy, I think he is just trying to cover up what he has done to those boys and that is our main objective here is to find them. But we can't under estimate him either, and he doesn't seem to be too smart in some ways or he wouldn't have kept that old truck after the shootout with us, seems he would have ditched it, but it's good for us he didn't. I hate to tell Lillian about the information about Alton we have, she will pick up on the fact of how dangerous he is and put two and two together and guess that Robert is no longer with us, but I hate to hide things from her either."

"Yeah", I said, "it is a tough call, you are damned if you do and damned if you don't but it is your call, Oscar."

"I know, think I will keep it to myself for now, unless she just totally pins me down and makes me tell all, which she can be very persuasive as we both know."

When we got to our house Ronnie was sitting on the front steps looking kind of lost, but trying not to show his fear for me, God, it's times like this I hate my work but at the same time I enjoy the excitement of it. Ronnie loves me very much, probably too much and only wants to protect me, but it always annoys me and he knows it so he tries not to be too upset over it. He put his arms around me and held me tight for just a second and then backed off a little but held tight to my hand until we had gotten into the house, which made me feel uncomfortable for just an instant.

He looked at me and said, "Do you think that this Carson man or both of the Carsons had something to do with the disappearance of the two boys and possibly their death?"

"Yeah, I would just about stake my life on it, but the next step is to prove it." and then he had fire in his eyes. He said, "But don't you think you should let the law handle it from here on in."

"But Ronnie you know I can't just quit in mid-stream until I get all the answers." He just walked off and shook his head in total disgust, oh well, marriage is for better or for worst, so I guess this is one of the worst times.

Well Thanksgiving is finally here and none too soon, but all the extra company and confusion and before, I had the bright idea since we were plagued with all the company, that we needed a new dinette set to accommodate everyone and it was delivered two days before Thanksgiving after the fight with the delivery guys, and who by the way couldn't speak any English and when they finally showed up after seven at night and missing one of the chairs that we had bought extra at a hundred and ten dollars each. I hit the roof, because they wanted us to sign the papers that we had received all the chairs even though we had not and they did not want to deliver the other one until the next day at seven o'clock at night and I refused, so I believe if I could have understood Spanish I would have found that he was giving me a severe cursing. But anyway after the cursing match I got the chair early the next morning. Actually everything went peaceful and Ladonna was on her best behavior with Ronnie's folks and only called Ronnie's mom a bitch once, but in a very low voice and hopefully it was not heard. In the afternoon Annie's two sisters-in-law from out of town came over to visit with all of us and that was a real experience. One of them is a widow and the other is a divorcee but quite a pair.

When they called for directions Ronnie got on the phone and tried to direct them to us and the one he talked to said we are lost so Ronnie asked her, "Where are you?" and her reply was in my car and he just rolled his eyes and sighed, but they finally made it and everyone seemed to have a nice day. Jonathon and Dirk didn't even get into another fight this year, maybe they are growing up, nah, just too many people to move around. Ronnie Jr. and his bunch went deer hunting after lunch and my daughter Annie and her new boyfriend and his two girls came over, but they left pretty early, probably if I had to guess because of her ex's sister's-in-laws coming over. They still consider Annie as family, even if she is no longer married to their brother, so I guess we are just one of those dysfunctional families you always hear about. Oh well. I guess it's better than no family, but sometimes I wonder about that one, so after everyone had gone except the ones that were here for the duration, or so it seemed, we set in to clean up the mess and freeze all the leftovers, which Ronnie and I always like to come in late and just heat and eat out of the freezer. Ronnie's folks had already decided to stay a while for an extended visit, which is always a pleasant surprise, but we just have to wear more clothes around the house when someone else is here, I guess we are just getting set in our ways and like our privacy, but also like to visit with them and get all the family gossip. After a game of Scrabble with Mandy, Ronnie and I went to bed still chuckling about his mom and dad necking in the living room when they thought we were not looking, but not really making fun, just surprised to see they are still that close after all those years of marriage, hope we stay that way. But with my line of work, no bets.

Chapter 22

The next morning after we said our goodbyes for the day, Ronnie was on his way to work. I called Oscar and told him to wait a while until he came to pick me up, that I had promised Mandy that I would come down and trim her hair a little, because she didn't have time to go to the salon before her trip to the shooting range for her practice run. I told her I couldn't go today because I explained that Oscar was my shadow for a while and gave her most of the details.

"Isn't this case getting a little dangerous?" she asked.

"Well, yeah, it is but it's like I told Ronnie I just can't back down now, because I am getting too close to the truth about those boys, but I'm damned if I'm going to be scared away that easily. Besides I have Oscar watching my back and I alerted Arnie and he is on his guard if I need to call for help."

"Well, I hope you have all the bases covered, and on a happier note would you and Ronnie like to go to a movie Saturday night with me? I promise I won't knee the guy beside me, even if he does step on my toe and get us thrown out."

"I will have to check with Ronnie and I don't think we should try and get back in to that same one for a while, we can go to the one on the other end of town, but try and not pick one that is an all gay movie." I said. "Ronnie was a little uncomfortable. Besides I will have to invite his folks, since they are still visiting, and they may be a little offended but I can't really understand why, it's a new world now, seems that everything goes these days, and we have to keep an open mind." When I looked out the window where there had been a squirrel running along the fence, I caught a shadow that definitely was not a limb. I guess my face went white and Mandy quietly got up and pulled her shot gun out of the corner and went to the window and the shadow made a sudden turn and seemed to disappear as fast as it appeared and the last thing I saw was Mandy pulling the trigger and yelling and running to the door, because I was out the window so fast I didn't see her change directions. Now this a wild side of Mandy most people don't see, but family and close friends know all too well how independent she can be and a tough old bird to boot. Well so much for a quiet morning with my neighbor, and as I looked up, here came Mandy's daughter and son-in-law with a hoe handle and a rake after the culprit and one of our neighbors with his big German Sheppard dog on a chain with fire in his eye. I almost felt sorry for the intruder at this point, but I said almost. He took off so fast I didn't see what he was driving or which way he went. But I bet he doesn't try that again unless this guy is really nuts. I called Oscar and told him what was going on and he was there in nothing flat, but was a little late to join in the gang attack. Well the only thing I accomplished this morning was I did get Mandy's hair finished. But I still wonder what happened to that poor squirrel on the fence, he probably keeled over with a heart attack.

Oscar and I went into town to my office so I could pull some of the notes we had taken down, I had the strangest feeling that I was missing something right in front of my face, and looked up and told him that something is just not adding up.

"Oscar", I said, "we need to see if we can talk to Regina's grandmother again and see if she can get the girl out of that house long enough for us to talk to her without Ernie around. I have the feeling she knows more than she is telling and may not realize that she knows it. But she is too scared to talk in front of her dad. What I need you to do is check and see when Ernie is not parked there at the house and let me know so I can get the grandmother, Meg, to try and get in touch with Regina to meet with her and us."

"Oscar", I said, "I'll stay here in the office the rest of the day and have Ladonna call Arnie and get him to come over, she says it's his day off and he can protect me as well as you can, after all he is a cop." Oscar got this hurt look on his face and started to argue with me, but decided it wouldn't do any good.

"Suzy, you are about the most aggravating woman I have ever known, but you are one of the toughest also, and good luck to Arnie for taking you off my hands this afternoon so I can have a break from your arrogant attitude. Ronnie is the bravest poor soul I have ever known to live with you and still have his sanity."

I just shook my fist at him and said, "I love you too, dear."

Meg answered on the fourth ring and as I was just about to hang up she said hello in her very sweet and polite voice I remembered so well, so southern sounding, and I explained that I wanted her to call Regina and set up a meeting anywhere she picked and she was delighted but expressed her concern for Regina and didn't want Ernie to do anything to hurt the child, and I assured her that I would take every precaution against that happening that I possibly could, and she finally agreed hesitantly. The trick was catching Regina at home alone and timing when we had to get her back, but only she could tell us when he would return, so this was going to be rather tricky. Meg was very nervous and was getting anxious to talk to her granddaughter and it was all I could do to keep her from calling her immediately. I told her it would probably not be today, unless she could arrange it so Regina would call her when Ernie was going to be out for a while, but it was getting late in the day and the weather was getting cold and drizzly and I was just about ready to hang it up for the day, and I knew the traffic was going to be bad because of the after Thanksgiving day sales going on. We decided it would be better to wait until next week to arrange the meeting. Meg wanted to do it now, but for good reason, because she hadn't seen her granddaughter in a long time, but finally she was ok with waiting.

After what seemed to be a long, long weekend with Ronnie's parents and Mandy and Ronnie and I going to the movies I thought it would never end, but it was a different way to spend our weekend, and the movie was pretty good that Mandy picked, at least we were not escorted to the door like the one before, darn, that was a little more exciting, but Ronnie didn't think so. After Ronnie heard about the incident over at Mandy's with the shot gun he stuck to me like glue all weekend, except when he was spreading manure in our garden in the freezing weather and wearing knee shorts with a heavy jacket, which was rather a sight for us country people and when Mandy came by he said she honked and whistled at him. He commented how crazy that woman was and I just looked him up and down with shorts on and said, "I am not so sure she is the only crazy one here, dolling." and he just winked at me and finished what he was doing.

I had brought the file home with me and asked Ronnie to look it over when he had a spare moment, maybe he could catch something I had overlooked and the first thing he asked was, “Isn't there a picture of a bunch of kids somewhere that you had?"

I remembered that I still had it in my purse. We laid it out on the kitchen table and he asked, "Now, where is the one you took similar to this one, but without the people in it." and I said I had it close to the back of the file, so I took it out and compared the two, and the one I took in the same place in the Carson's back yard the day I was back there snooping around had something else that wasn't there when the first picture was taken. It never occurred to me that there was something different besides just the kids not being in the picture. There was a hot tub in the one I took and not in the one with the kids in front of the pool.

I said, "I knew there was something right in front of my face, but I couldn't put my finger on it. I remember thinking that these people have a lot of excess money to spend if they can give their kids pools and hot tubs for their recreation."

Ronnie said, "Maybe this has something to do with your case."

"Wait a minute, let me pull the tax records I got from the court house and see if there were any improvements in the last year or so." So we looked up the form in the file folder and there it was bigger than life itself.

"Big difference", I said, "you see what I see, Ronnie? Yeah, this was added on not too long ago, just about a year and a half ago. What a big jump in their taxes and they even bought permits to have it installed, and living that far out of town they wouldn't have to get an inspector out."

Then Ronnie got a strange look on his face and said, "You don't think..."

"Whoah there", I yelled and held up my hand, "let's don't get too far ahead of ourselves because speculating and proving are two very different things, but we will notify Arnie and Oscar of what we have discovered and see what they think we should do next." So I called Oscar and told him about the hot tub and he said he would call me back later, that he wanted to think about it for a while, and go over something, and just before we went to bed he called back and said he was curious about that receipt from the concrete company now at the Morrison's house he had found and wondered if there was any connection.

Chapter 23

By the next morning I was so wound up and kind of worried about what we found in the file that I could hardly wait for Oscar to get there, so I sat out on the steps and waited for him, and even Ronnie was kind of excited about everything and he wouldn't leave before Oscar came for me. When Oscar drove up, he saw Ronnie with me having coffee and had a puzzled look on his face, and said, “This is a first, you two really are a couple, I was beginning to think you were just faking it”, then said, “Where's my coffee?” and Ronnie just waved him off and told him to close his lip and get his own blasted coffee if he wanted any. Those two act more like they are married than Ronnie and I do, the way they argue back and forth.

Oscar said, “I will go back to Lillian's later this afternoon and see if Ernie Carson leaves at any time after Regina comes back from school.

I said, “Oscar don't you know about the school system, the kids are still out for Thanksgiving vacation until Thursday, this is only Monday. I will get Meg to call Regina and see if her dad is working, and let’s just hope he isn't on vacation also. And Oscar, call Lillian and see if we can set up the meeting over at her house since she lives just a few doors down from the Carson's, and that way if Ernie comes home unexpectedly Regina can tell him she went to the neighbors to borrow some sugar or something, and he won’t be as rough on her as he would if she left the neighborhood.”

“Good idea”, he said, “but you think the grandmother will agree to meet her without taking her out somewhere?"

"I think so", I said, "if she has no choice and as bad as she wants to see her, she will agree to just about any terms. Also, I think we should let the police in on what we are going to do."

Oscar said, "Not yet, but I'll alert Arnie so if anything goes wrong he will be on standby and maybe come over closer to the area."

"Sounds like you have it all worked out, genius", Ronnie butted in saying, "Yeah, all but what will happen to Regina if she knows anything and starts talking about it. But as I went on to say, I think Ernie will protect her from Alton, and he has done a pretty good job of it so far, now protecting her from Ernie is going to be another matter entirely, but we will cross that bridge when we come to it. The next problem at hand is where Alton is, he seems to have dropped out of sight for now, but you can bet that was him at Mandy's house and with that shotgun of hers around I bet he doesn't come around here for a while.

Oscar said, "Don't count on it, you know how crazy he is, and if he was brave enough to kill his own mother and sister, as I suspect, he is not going to quibble when it comes to getting rid of one of us. So we all have to be very cautious."

"I can't believe the police haven't picked up on any of this", I said, "but on the other hand they are not going to share information with us, so they probably have." I went on to say, "That's probably why he is in hiding."

We left the house and started over to Lillian's to try and set up the meeting there, since she was off on Thanksgiving vacation, what's up with this, I didn't get a break. Well my only break is entertaining family, but it could be worse, I could still be working for the company I left, boy what a horrible thought, and I shivered all over just thinking of it.

By the time we had reached Lillian's, Meg's car was already in the driveway. Boy that was quick, and she had already called Regina immediately after our conversation, I guess. Ernie was at work, it seems, and it was early yet, so we had most of the day and I was excited about this, in one way, but dreading it in another. I knew this was going to be hard for Regina, and probably be earth shattering to her as her whole world unravels in front of her. After all, this is her father and half-brother that look very guilty at this moment, and I am not sure she will understand what has happened. When it all comes to light I am afraid of what her reaction will be, but luckily Meg will be around to help her to pick up the pieces of her life.

Lillian came to the door to meet us and to give Oscar, the ladies man, a little love pat on the toosh, and he just smiled real big like a big old dumb teddy bear. I looked at him with a scowl on my face and said, "Now if we can get down to business."

Meg stood when I came in and said she had called Regina and said that she would join us in a few minutes. When she knocked on the door Meg almost ran over Lillian to answer the door, and grabbed Regina as if she had not seen her in a long time, which to her I guess it was.

She asked, "Why did you want me to come over to Roberts's house, Grandmother? I don't want to be over here." and she got a scared look on her face and Lillian looked hurt to hear this, but didn't say anything to her.

Oscar looked toward me and was a little confused of what had just happened, and I stood up and said, "If you would be more comfortable at your grandmother's house, then we can talk there, I just didn't know how much time we had before you had to be back home. I would rather go to grandmother's house, than here or maybe go over to Sabrina's next door and I am sure it will be ok, we can call her from here." Oscar and I still had a puzzled look on our face, if I was to guess, because this did not have a good feel to it for Regina not to want to stay in Robert's and Lillian's house. But if we were going to get anywhere with her she had to feel comfortable and it was obvious that she was very nervous and almost hostile to be here, so we all moved the meeting over to Sabrina's, and her mom welcomed all of us to traipse through her house.

Chapter 24

Mrs. Lane asked everyone if they would like something hot to drink, since it was so cold and windy out, to warm the bones, she said, and we all shook our heads no.

"We really need to get started here", I said, "Regina, I would like to ask you some questions about Robert, and by the way why were you so adamant about not wanting to talk over at Lillian's. Do you have a problem with her?"

"Oh no", she said, quickly, "Mrs. Chambers is very nice but I just don't want to talk in front of her." and she began to cry, and in an instant Meg had her arm around her, the protective grandmother as she is, and I would have done the same thing had it been one of mine.

"Regina do you know something about Robert's disappearance that you haven't told the police? I get the feeling you are hiding something."

"If my dad finds out", she shouted, "I am afraid of what he will do to me. Not so much Dad as Alton."

I pulled up a chair from the corner of the room and got closer so I could talk directly to her, and asked, "What are you so afraid of, child?"

She began to cry harder, then she said, "I am afraid they did something to them."

I asked, "To who, Regina, what are you talking about, Robert?"

She shook her head yes and said, "And Jesse, but I don't know for sure I just have this horrible feeling deep down after that night and what happened that maybe Dad called Alton, and I know how much my dad hates Robert."

"What happened on the night in question?" I asked. "Did Robert and Jesse hurt you in any way?"

"I guess you could say they did mentally, I am almost afraid to go out of the house any more except to school. Robert was totally different when Jesse was around, he got mean, as if he were showing off for him or as if he were trying to impress him, but I was not hurt physically, but they just about scared me to death. I was inside the house when I heard someone trying to turn the door knob but it was locked and secured with the chain on. My dad always gave me strict orders to lock everything safely. When dad left I decided to do some sewing, so I went to the back of the house and from there I saw car lights as they pulled into the drive way. Since I was alone I didn't answer the door and then my hands began to tremble thinking about who it could be, possibly Alton, and my dad always told me not to let him in at all. But my thoughts turned around, when I heard Robert call out in a loud and nasty sounding voice and then Jesse yelled for me to open the door, and called me a bitch. Both of them sounded as if they were drinking or something, or maybe smoking pot, which they did sometimes. Robert said for me to open the door, you bitch and I started screaming for them to go away, but they acted like crazy people, so I turned out the light on the end table next to the door, and just huddled down near the floor. After a few minutes they changed tactics on me and went around to the side of the house to the window, but it was locked, and I was so sure they were going to throw something through it, but instead, one of them headed for the front door and the other went around to the back one and started beating on them. I was shaking all over by then and crying so hard I seemed to be out of control with fear but I decided I had to tough it out and try to get help. It sounded as if one of them had something heavy, like a baseball bat or tire iron maybe, beating on the front door and the other just kept kicking the other one. I can't believe I had been so wrong about Robert and cared for him as I did, but you never know how people will react to drugs and alcohol. I finally made my way down the hall and managed to get my cell phone and dial 911. The lady on the phone stayed on the line with me until the police arrived, and it didn't take long for the sirens to get close enough for the intruders to hear them, and they zoomed out of there so fast the tires were squealing. As the police drove up so did my dad, with this horrified look on his face, and he looked at me and shook his head as if to let me know that I was not to give too much information about what was going on. So I briefly told them that two boys had tried to break in to the house while I was alone, but did not really get a good look at them, which was probably the wrong thing to do, but I was more afraid of my dad than I was of them. After they left, my dad gave me the third degree and wanted to know who the boys were, and I had a bad feeling of what he was going to do, but I had no choice at this point, and he said he would take care of it."

Sabrina sat very quietly, but stayed by Regina's side through the whole ordeal of her telling the story of what happened that night and just kept trying to assure her that we were all here for her, boy, that is a true friend, I was thinking, and Meg, her grandmother was on the other side partially holding her, and trying to be as loving as she could without being too pushy, but Regina didn't take it that way at all, she was just so glad her grandmother was by her side and comforting her at this moment. I think we all got a little teary eyed. Regina finally said, "I would like a coke, Mrs. Lane if I could, please, my mouth is so dry and I am still shaking, just thinking of what all has happened."

I asked, "Regina do you know how long it was after the attempted break-in at your house that you heard of Robert's disappearance?"

She kind of looked like she wanted to cry again, and then sucked in a deep breath, and replied, "I believe it was in the same month, but I don't remember exactly how many actual days it was. I do remember thinking that my dad was involved somehow, and my dad is a really good person deep down, but sometimes he acts like two different people, especially when he goes around Alton. I truly believe Alton is an evil person through and through."

"Then you think he has been in touch with Alton lately?" I asked.

"I am almost positive he had been, right after the incident with Robert, because he was in that agitated mood he gets into after he is around him, so I am pretty sure they had been in touch when he came home that day."

"Regina, do you have any idea where Alton is staying here in Houston? We do know that his mother left him the old home place in Alabama", I said, "but he has fled there since it has been discovered."

Her face changed colors immediately as she shook her head no. She looked so frightened again, but tried not to let us know. When she looked back up at me, I felt so sorry that we were putting her through all this, but I was so sure now that we had a super big murder case in our hands and Oscar looked at me and made a quiet and mock whistling motion, as if he were reading my mind and thinking the same thing I was. He just shook his head and rolled his eyes around to get my attention and motioned for me to follow him.

We stepped into the kitchen as if to get something to drink and Oscar said, "Wow, what do you make of all of this? I know she is telling us it like it is, but where do we go from here?"

"Well", I said, "first thing we do is contact the police again and report the conversation, but it wouldn't hold up in court, it's hearsay."

"Yeah, but we should have at least been recording the conversation", he said and I just stood there with nothing to add, and Oscar got this big grin on his face and said, "You didn't?" and I pulled the portable recorder out of my jeans pocket. Oscar said, "I should have known, but you know that the recording would probably not be allowed in court either."

"I know, but it will make the police listen, and take us a little more serious than they have been and at least when we go in with this, they won't just tell me I have a big imagination. And by the way, I did tell Meg what I was going to do before the fact, and she agreed it was a good idea, also, and that it might help Regina."

Chapter 25

After all the excitement was over I told Regina she should go back home before Ernie returned, but she wanted to visit with her grandmother a bit longer and explained that Ernie was not due back for a while yet. Oscar left us and went back over to Lillian's to explain some of what was said, but there is a fine line between divulging too much information to a client and not quite enough, but in this case the client was the mother of the missing person and the mother of a possible law breaker that was punished too severely, probably with his life. I felt very confident that Oscar would handle it in the best way possible, without being too harsh, and this is the reason you don't want to be personally involved in a case. After the dust settled as they say, Regina and Sabrina talked and tried to catch up on old friends and school gossip. Meg said her goodbyes, but did not really want to leave her granddaughter so soon. As for me I joined Oscar over at Lillian's and as I expected she had a lot of questions for me and all I could think of was getting home and enjoying the peace and quiet of my own living room but as usual that was just a pretense in my own mind.

Lillian was trying to figure out why Robert would do such a thing like that and she stopped and said, "That poor child, she had to be so frightened. What could Robert have been thinking, even though he and Jesse were such good friends I didn't know they were capable of this kind of harassment, but then I guess I didn't know Jesse very well at all? I should have been more observant of what and who Robert was involved in, but we get so wrapped up in everyday life that so many of the important things of life seem to get swept under the rug."

Oscar held up his hand for her to stop, and said, "You can't blame yourself for his actions and bad judgment when you are not always around, everyone is responsible for their own actions."

I looked at her and said, "Yes, he is right, you know, we raise them the best we know how and hope for the best."

On the way back home Oscar and I didn't have much to say to each other, but I still had the feeling we were missing something.

"Well", he said, "everything Regina told us adds up to revenge for what the boys put her through, but we have the task of proving it, or sit back and let Alton or Ernie come to us, and they will, you know."

"I know, it is just the matter of where and when."

"Is there some way we can make them do it faster, maybe dangle some bait in front of them, and wrap this up?" I asked.

"Well if we or the police start harassing Ernie, he will probably get in touch with Alton and they will try to solve the problem, with our necks, so we have to be ready for them. By the way, Suzy, I talked to Joan Morrison, and she said she would try and find that receipt from the concrete company and call us at the office. In all the excitement I forgot to tell you, so you could check at the office with Ladonna and see if she had called."

"This is a great time to tell me, but we can swing by the office on the way to the house", I said.

"Do I really have to come face to face with that bitch sister of yours?" Oscar asked.

"Yeah, I will play referee, but don't intimidate her."

and he let out a snort and said, “Me intimidate her! It's the other way around.”

Ladonna was about to leave for the day when we got there, which was good for Oscar and as she handed me the messages, she gave him a snidey look, that could have frosted over a snowball, and he just grinned her way with fire in his eye. One of the messages was from Joan, and she was sorry she couldn't find the receipt from the concrete company. Why am I not surprised, it was most likely taken when George was killed, but that was no reason for murder, unless he walked in on the prowler.

"Ok, Oscar I want to know when that hot tub was delivered at the Carson's and who installed it."

When I finally made it home Ronnie and his folks had gone out to dinner but left me a note to meet them in town. Well, I missed that one by about an hour or so, but as I guessed he would, Ronnie brought me a doggy bag that was a full dinner and said he had tried to reach me all day to tell me about dinner. He seemed a little chapped over it, but got over it quickly when he needed me to give him a full body massage, later that night. But before we went to bed, I gave him a rundown of what all Regina had to tell us and filled him in on what was mostly speculation, on our part, all but the part of setting a trap for the killer or killers. No use in adding fuel to the fire, and have him worry any more than he does.

The next morning I asked Mandy if she wanted to go to the shooting range with me, and I knew that was a foolish question, she is always ready to exercise her weapons but I didn't know if maybe she already had plans. We got in a little practice and I dropped her off and went back home, and waited for Oscar to pick me up. He managed to get the name of the contractor that set the hot tub in for Ernie but never did find him to talk with him. Another among the missing. This is beginning to really stink to me, no loose ends anywhere.

"Oscar, you know if our plan is to work we have to split up, which means I take my car and not let Ernie see us together, but to let him think that I am on my own again."

"Yeah, I know", he said, "but Ronnie is not going to go for that without putting up a fight."

"Yeah, well I'll handle him but just don't stay back too far from the action."

"You know I will always be two steps behind to make sure that nothing happens, because I sure don't want to go job hunting right here at Christmas time." and he winked. Boy, that really makes me feel all cozy inside. Oscar has such a way with words that can really get to me sometimes, but he is not only a partner, but also a friend and knows how to make me feel safe. He looked up and said, "You know Suzy, maybe I should call some reinforcements in to make sure that we have all our bases covered?"

"Who did you have in mind?" I asked.

"Let me check with Goofy Larry Wade, from the gym and his brother Wally."

"Oh Lord, not those two, the last time they helped out we had every con man in town calling me to work for them because they spread the word that they were acquainted with a private eye, and aren't they the ones that their mom got picked up for lifting the mayor's watch out of his pocket in a bar?"

"Yeah, but they are great with a gun and are pretty good strong arm men."

I looked at him straight in the eye, and asked, "Don't you know any honest and decent people?"

"Yeah, but the ones I know can't shoot straight, and wouldn't do us any good if we got in a tight spot."

So Oscar and I separated and went different directions, or so it seemed and our body guards were somewhere out of sight I hoped. My first stop was to the office to check in with Ladonna and make sure Arnie and his bunch knew we were out and about. Ladonna had a bright red full length and baggy shirt and tight leotards under it with red six inch heels and a big red head band to match and looked like a big red bird that had burst into flames. I had to turn around and do a double take. She just shot me a go to hell look and went and sat down at her desk.

I said, "What are you dressed up for, Halloween has already come and went." But I guess she didn't feel that my question deserved an answer and so she didn't bother.

She sort of looked disgusted with me and said, "You wear what you want and I will do the same. At least I don't look like I shop at the Army surplus store." she said. "Oh, I almost forgot, Suzy, someone left this note for you under the door this morning."

I opened it immediately, knowing just about what it said, but I didn't know it would be so explicit. I guess my face must have turned different colors, because Ladonna got up and took it out of my hand and looked at it and put her hand over her mouth to keep from letting out a yell. But she gasped and asked, "Who in the world did you piss off to the point that they want to do this evil thing to you. I always said you would lose your head over something, but I didn't mean it literally and then have it hanging on a pole is a little excessive."

"Well", I said, "this case we are working on is getting pretty close to getting solved and I believe we are looking for some horrible people."

"I'll say." she said. Then, she walked right over to the phone on her desk and called Arnie to come immediately, and told him it was an emergency. The police station is a pretty good ways from the office, but he got there in a flash. In the time it took him to get there Oscar had made it first. I just had to let him know what was happening, and hoped he wouldn't call Ronnie, but he did and didn't even try to make excuses this time. Ronnie came in steaming and the first thing he did was turn on Oscar and ask him what in the hell was I doing running around by myself. I jumped in to the argument before it got heated up and threw my hand up and told him that it was my idea. The only way we are going to smoke them out is to separate and make them think that I am on my own, so they will make their move. He wasn't happy about it but he knew I was right, and he just walked outside as if to leave in a heat of anger, so I followed him out the door and caught his arm, but when he turned to look at me I could see extreme fear in his eyes, he always knew how to melt my heart, so I mellowed out a little, and said, "I know this has been a bad time for us, but I just can't leave this unfinished."

He said, "I know, Suzy, but I can't even think about losing you to some crazy man that probably wouldn't even think twice of killing anyone who gets in his way. I don't think I could handle not having you around to needle me day and night. So, please be careful, and at least let me take part in trapping them, or something to help, so I don't feel so damn helpless."

"Ok, just don't stay too close on my heels and scare them off." and with that said, he gave me a big sloppy kiss that I thought I would need a towel to wipe my face afterwards. Ronnie and I went back into the office and the others stared at us but said nothing.

Finally Oscar spoke up to break the ice chill in the room and said, "Well, are things back to normal in crazy land with you two?" and I said for him to give it a rest, that we had a lot of work to do and that Ronnie was to be included for sure this time. That statement seemed to calm him down even more, so maybe he wouldn't feel so bad about the whole Ernie and Alton thing now.

"Ladonna, how did this note come?" I asked.

"It was just on the floor, I guess someone just slipped it under the door. It was there when I got here this morning, but we can call around the complex and see if anyone saw who might have left it there. Security will a be a good place to start." and she picked up the phone and called them, which as she put it was a waste of time, no one saw anything it seems, but she didn't stop there and called some of her buddies that man the phones for other businesses and one of the girls remembered a shabby old truck parked in front of our office but didn't see who was in it or if they got out. Another dead end, or maybe not, because one of the girls called back and said she went out to get coffee and saw a burley looking, fairly young man walking away from our door and that he seemed to be in a bit of a hurry. I went over there and showed her the picture of Alton and she confirmed it. Now we are getting somewhere, and I walked back and told Arnie to see if he could have him picked up for giving out malicious threats of bodily harm and he said that was not a legal complaint unless a handwriting expert was called out and a lot of red tape to go through, which could take forever and he could do a lot of damage in that length of time, but that they would get him in for questioning, and maybe that will scare him off or piss him off enough to come gunning for you full force, and we can catch him in the act.

"We sure need to get this psycho off the streets, and fast. I am going to try and get you some protection while we wait for him to make a move, so try to lay low a few days, and don't give him a chance to get at you."

I raised my hand at him, and said, "Look Arnie, I'll tell you as I told Ronnie, that the whole point of all this is to make enough waves so he will try and get at me, so we can take him down, and have all this behind us. If I just lay low as you said he won't try an attempt on my life and we are back to square one."

"But", he said, "that is the same as using yourself as bait and I won't allow it, because what you don't understand is, is that this guy is as crazy as they come and you don't need to take any unnecessary chances."

And about that time Ronnie looked my way and said, "That's just what I have been telling you, Suzy, but you are right about one thing, the sooner we catch him the sooner we can all get back to normal, whatever that is any more."

"So you are on my side?"

I grinned at him as he sneered at me and said, "I am always on your side but there is not any use in taking chances with yours or anyone else's lives, ok?"

"Yeah, I said I get it, but let's see if we can come up with an idea to smoke him out and snag him."

Chapter 26

Oscar was not saying too much after Ronnie reamed him out over letting me come in alone, but finally he asked Ronnie if they were still buddies, and Ronnie sheepishly replied, “Yeah, sorry I blew up at you man, but this stuff is making me crazy, I don't see how you people do this every day without losing it, I guess that's the reason I'm not in that line of work. No, that's not the reason, I don't have the nerves for this."

Oscar said, “Yeah some days it gets to us, too, when things turn like it has the last few days but you have to ride it out until it gets better, or worse, which ever the case may be."

"It pays off in the end, and at the end of the day we rest a little easier knowing we have done our part for society." Oscar said with a gloating grin. I'm not sure Ronnie bought all that bull, but he seemed a little more satisfied that Oscar took the time to stop to explain things in a more professional way than usual. Which maybe he meant every word of it, but knowing him I wouldn't want to bet on it.

"What do you say we call it a day and all go and get a beer and some dinner?”

Oscar said, “Hey, Suzy do we have to invite your sister dressed in that get up she has on? Arnie is great, but I'm not sure I want to be seen with her dressed like that.”

“Oscar be nice, you know we can't ask one without the other, and after all she is one of the gang now since she works with us, but maybe we will luck out and she will say no.”

As luck would have it she and Arnie accepted, but to my surprise she went and changed into jeans and a tee shirt and looked somewhat like the rest of us, which was not all that great but acceptable. When we left the office I could tell Ronnie was nervous and looking all around but I happened to look out across the street in front of the bar-b-q joint here in town where we get our take outs from time to time, and saw what I guess was a police man or one of Oscar's buddies playing bodyguard. Arnie said it wasn't one of theirs, so I sure hoped it was one of the goofus brothers. Oscar then did a half salute to him and I felt somewhat calmer about it in a not so fuzzy feeling way. But just the same I didn't feel that we were just stuck out there as practice targets either.

"Does Malone's Bar and Grill sound ok or do you have another suggestion?" I asked all, and everyone agreed that it would be ok, informal and relaxed and a laid back atmosphere that we all needed. We all met there in separate vehicles except Ronnie made me leave my car at the office and ride with him, not a big surprise, but I guess it only shows he cares what happens to me. Oscar called Lillian and invited her to meet us and she was delighted that she didn't have to cook but probably would have been happier with a little more notice ahead of time. Malone's was pretty crowded, after all it was early evening, and the after work and happy hour bunch was loud and rowdy. Our usual waitress, Bonita, greeted us as we walked in and seated us at the end of the bar at a huge booth right under a heater vent, which felt great after coming in out of the chilled evening. Aah, I thought, we can finally unwind after a day's aggravation, I thought it would never come.

The conversation soon turned to the case and Oscar clued Lillian in on what was happening and she didn't take it very well, she turned to me and I saw tears, and she asked very shakily, "What have I gotten you into, Suzy? I never meant for it to come to this with you right in the middle. Maybe you should walk away now and hopefully the people involved will let it go also." but she knew the answer, before I even spoke.

"Lillian, you know I can't do that. We are too close, that is why I am being threatened. By the way it's not the first time and I'm sure it won't be the last either, so rest assured I will handle it. There are too many things that have happened to let it go now and we still haven't found Robert."

"I know you are right, but if anything happens to you or Oscar or anyone involved I will never forgive myself, so if you won't quit I suppose I could dismiss you from the case but you wouldn't give it up, would you?"

"No", I said, "I'm too close now, so even if you cut us loose I'm not backing down until I've solved this case."

"That's what I thought, so carry on then and I'll butt out and let you handle it. Ok, now let's not talk about the case anymore and have a relaxing evening."

Every one agreed and Oscar started needling Ladonna about the outfit she wore today, and they ended up in a cursing match between them that Arnie and I had to break up. What an evening to remember.

The next morning was cold and dreary, and Ronnie had to leave early to lead his folks out to the edge of town so they could head home. They decided to cut their trip a little short, because Ronnie's dad had a doctor's appointment. He started to feel bad and called in to his doctor, and was told to get in to the office as soon as he could. They said they would not be back for Christmas, that they had already made plans to go on a ski trip with friends. Christmas, gee, I need to finish my shopping, so I guess I need to call one of my body guards to escort me. I did not want to go shopping with just anyone, so I finally talked Oscar into tagging along, boy what a mistake that was. He is worse than Ronnie is about shopping and rushing me. I asked Oscar if he and Lillian would like to join us and the kids for our Christmas dinner and gathering and he declined. Smart fellow, I am jealous because I don't have a choice in the matter.

Well, Christmas came and went and was one of the most peaceful ones we have had in a long time, no fights or insults to each other, and everyone seemed to get everything they requested, even the grand kids seemed to be pretty happy with everything they got. Boy what a surprise that was, they never cease to amaze me. But it seemed the thought of Lillian spending the holidays wondering if she would ever spend another one with her child just kept haunting me and sort of made me a little sad and guilty about having mine this time of year even if they are annoying some time, but they can be just as loving at other times.

The next day I called Oscar to come and pick me up to go to the office and just mostly kill time waiting for Alton to make a move and at this point I was getting a little nervous and edgy. Oscar would never admit it but I think he was also a little unsettled about the waiting because he seemed too quiet for him which is a rarity or maybe a blessing in disguise.

We made small talk into town and I turned and asked Oscar, "Do you think Lillian will ever be the same if she finds out that Robert is not coming back to her? I don't think I could handle it but maybe she is a much stronger person than I am."

"I think with all of us here to give her daily support and just be there for her she will handle it fine." he said. "And, yes she is a real strong one, and we just have to make sure that these sickos pay for what they have done. It surely won't bring Robert back, but maybe it will bring her some comfort to know that they are off the streets."

There was still a bit of a chill in the air, and I just seemed to keep shaking, even with the heater going full blast. When we got to the office Ladonna was just making coffee and looking fresh as a daisy, which was not stretching it a bit, in her daisy white and yellow outfit with matching hair band and yellow shoes. Oscar just shook his head in disgust and rolled his eyes back and grunted loud enough for Ladonna to turn around swiftly and caught him square in the crotch with the hot coffee, just enough to get his attention and almost a slap in her direction as he caught himself, and just about that time, I stepped in between them to break it up.

"You two act like children, instead of adults, and are getting on my last nerve, so just cut the crap and go to your own corners of the office."

Ladonna handed me messages from the day before and a cup of coffee and just grunted toward Oscar and went back to her desk. About that time I heard a knock on the door, which was very strange, because a business like ours has an open door policy, and you just walk in. So Oscar and I were both very suspicious, and a little surprised. He stood behind the door while I had my pistol in hand and he slowly opened the door as I stood back out of sight just in case someone was there to barge in or start shooting. But to our surprise no one was there, just a statue of a Dutch girl on the floor that I'll bet was the one that belonged to Alton's mother that was stolen from Lillian's neighbor George, the night he was killed.

I looked at Oscar and said, “Just another piece of the sordid puzzle of this weird case.” and I reminded him of the statue that was missing from George’s house.

“Ok”, Oscar said, “I've just about had all of this mysterious shit I can stand, let’s go make Ernie tell us where Alton is and beat a confession out of the both of them."

"Yeah Oscar, get back in the real world with the rest of us now. This is just their way of gradually coming out in the open, which is exactly what we want them to do. So sit tight and let them come to us and then we can put them away where they belong. Besides the statue was the one that belonged to Alton's mother so it's not so mysterious. He is just letting us know that he was the one in George's house and he was the one that killed him, and he wants us to know it for sure to scare us. The statue is his proof that he was there. It's just another one of his scare tactics that's not going to work anymore than the rest of them he has used."

Chapter 27

After the little episode at the office we drove out to Ernie's and no one was home, so we decided to meet Ronnie for a beer and head on our separate ways. I rode home with Ronnie and explained the events of the day, and as usual he was not happy about all that happened, but he tried not to be too cranky about things. I could tell he was just worried about me, so I left it alone.

The next morning the weather looked nasty and cold, so after Ronnie left for work I crawled back into the warmth of our bed and dozed another hour. After my shower I went down to the kitchen to have my morning coffee and saw the back door was slightly ajar, and a cold chill went down my neck, I knew at that instant that I was not alone, and about that time I caught a glimpse of Ernie stepping out of my utility room just off the side of the kitchen.

I tried to break and run but he moved faster and caught me with a strong arm around my neck, then he stuck a gun in my ribs and said, “Ok little lady let’s take a quick ride and end this, for you anyway. You were warned time and time again, but you just wouldn't take the hint, so now it's too late, no more talking. You want to know where those two boys are so bad, well you will soon join them. Now let’s go.” he said as he shoved me out the door. I tried to keep a cool head, but knew he had probably killed before and would not think twice about pulling that trigger. So I did what I was told and didn't make any quick moves for the moment but was constantly thinking how I might get myself out of this mess.

As we entered Ernie's back yard, I had the eeriest feeling that we were not alone, and I turned around just in time to see Alton bring a shovel down on my shoulder and I fell to the ground so hard that I felt my jaw bone crack and my teeth rattle. I was still conscious enough to hear a shotgun blast and Alton grab his chest and he fell to the ground without making a sound. But who shot him and from where, I thought? Just before everything went black I saw Mandy bending over me and shaking me and trying to revive me, with no luck and with a frightened look on her face, but where did she come from? By the time I regained consciousness the whole gang was around me and cops were running in all directions and Ernie was in handcuffs and screaming that they had killed his son. Mandy was by my side through the whole ordeal and trying to comfort me and rubbing my hand as if to make it all better. Gotta love her. The medics were trying to put me in a shoulder sling and said that my jaw was broken and needed to be set, and that they were taking me to the hospital. Ronnie wasn't sure if he wanted to hug me or break the other jaw, but decided I had been injured enough for one day and didn't say anything, but looked terrified and very distraught.

I yelled at Ronnie, as best as I could with a broken jaw, “Ronnie”, I said, “don't let the medics take me yet, help me up and get me over near the hot tub, and look and see if there is a hole dug close to it, I have to know.”

“Suzy you really need to go to the hospital.” and I held up my hand and waved for Oscar to come over.

“Oscar, look over and see if there is fresh dirt or a hole. Ernie said I was going to join the two boys soon, and according to the records that hot tub went up about the time the boys disappeared.”

He looked at me with terror and fear on his face and said, “You don't mean they buried them under the hot tub?"

"Yeah, I will bet the bank that they are under there and I wish I were wrong but I'll bet I'm not. That hole dug, if there is one was meant for me, I'm sure, these guys were very thorough and thought of everything except that there was a crazy old woman running loose with a shotgun, and I was probably spared because of her."

Mandy came back over to see how I was and I asked, "How did you know I was here?"

"I had to take my grandson to school and saw a strange car with a man in it, that I didn't recognize, and when I came back by, the car was still there, so I went back home and got my shot gun and waited and followed the two of you here. I saw he had a gun on you so I figured he wasn't a friendly visitor. When I went back home for my gun I called Arnie, and also told him to call Ronnie, but Arnie said they didn't want to scare them off, they wanted to end this thing once and for all, so he and the others would hold back a short distance and when they heard my gun fire, then they came a running but I was not about to hold back with those two killers and I came in the back way without them seeing me."

"And none too soon obviously", I said and I tried to hug her but couldn't move too well. She had an idea what I felt at this moment.

"The one you shot, Mandy, Alton, is he alive?"

"No", she said, "his chest was shattered and he died instantly."

"Where is Ginny?" I asked in a low voice and near tears, but very concerned.

"The lady down the road took her to her house to call her grandmother, and they are all over there."

"What lady?" I asked feeling my stomach twist in a million knots, and Oscar answered quickly.

"It was Lillian." he said seeing by the look on my

face how worried I was.

"So she doesn't know about the boys?" I asked quickly.

"No, I want to be damn sure before I say anything and by the way you were right on the nose about the hole near the hot tub. I'll get Arnie to start working on having that thing dug up, and see what's under there. Ernie also has a lot of questions to answer, and they will charge him with kidnapping with intent to murder. So he will never see daylight again, I'm sure of it. Now Suzy, let us handle this and you go and see what damage was done to you, and Ladonna is on the way to the hospital."

"Great, as if I'm not already in enough misery." and Oscar had to laugh out loud at that one as he walked off.

When we got to the hospital Ladonna was already there waiting for me, with tears streaming down like a water fall, so I assured her I was not hurt that bad, she finally calmed down some before they took me into surgery but I'm sure she gave the doctors hell until they gave her some information about what was going on in the operating room. That was all I remembered until the next morning and Ronnie was asleep in the chair beside me and Ladonna was asleep at the foot of my bed. The nurse came in and everyone jumped nearly out of their skin and were amazed that I was already awake and not exactly smiling with my jaw wired up and my armed bandaged.

After a few minutes of waking up, I asked Ronnie, "Have you heard from Arnie on whether they have started digging up that back yard yet?"

"Yeah, and he said he would know more later today and would be in to talk to you about it all."

Tears started to fall just like a big old baby and I asked if Lillian knew what we suspected.

Ronnie held me close and said, "Oscar says she has a feeling about it more than anything but is trying to put on a good front mostly so she doesn't fall apart. She says if it is possible for the heart to hurt, then that was the way she felt, like her heart was breaking, so she has an idea the boys are dead in that back yard."

Just after I finished asking about Lillian, she and Oscar came into my room, very concerned and she started fussing over me and propping my pillow up and wanting to know if there was anything she could do and that she felt that this was all her fault. She and Oscar asked how the jaw was, and Oscar pulled out a stick of gum for me and we all had a good laugh. Lillian took my hand and said, "At least, now I know where Robert is, and that he did not just run away. Just as we were leaving", she continued, "the police came by and informed me that they had found the remains of two people buried under the hot tub and that they found Robert's wallet with his driver's license in it", and her voice was beginning to quiver a bit. It kept going through my mind that, Lord this woman had been through a lot. I began to cry harder now and she bent down and hugged me and said, "I always had a feeling in the back of my mind that this was a possibility of what might have happened but would not give into the idea of it until we knew for sure. So don't you feel so bad about it, at least you gave me the answers I needed and almost lost your life in the process."

Oscar broke in about that time, before we all lost it and said, "Ernie gave a complete confession and explained all the details of the murders in this folder Arnie sent for you. He will be in later to take your statement and wrap up the loose ends of the case."

There was a knock on the door and Ronnie opened it for Mandy, and the whole gang started hoorahing for her.

"Woman, you know you saved the day, not to mention saving my old butt, I wanted to thank you again straight from the heart."

"I never let you out of my sight the whole time after I saw you were taken at gun point." she explained. At least not until we reached the short cut where I turned off of the main road to get there before you and that's when I spotted the other one waiting back in the shadows and I just had a feeling he was up to no good."

"Well", Ronnie piped up, trying to lighten the mood in the room, and said in a shaky voice, "we owe you big time, maybe we can buy you a new shot gun or something."

"You don't owe me anything, it's just that I'm too old to hunt for new friends, so I have to look after the ones I have." And she got the biggest grin on her face at that one.

After everyone but Ronnie and Ladonna left I tried to look over the file that Arnie had sent me and it was so sad to read how Ernie described how they walked the two boys into the woods as they held a rifle on them and the thought of what the boys must have been thinking as they were about to die, and I was thinking, so young for their lives to end that way. It was just more than I could take, so I threw it down on the bed and looked up and said, "I feel so bad for Lillian." trying to talk with the wire in my jaw, and then I began to cry uncontrollably, but I managed to say, "At least maybe she can have some closure to all of this." Ronnie and Ladonna both put their arms around me and began to cry too.

Epilogue

After everything settled down I called Meg, Regina's grandmother and she said that she and Regina were leaving for an extended vacation in Europe so Regina could have a little R and R and try to mend all the bad feelings she had for her father for letting things get as far as they did but that she said after all he was still her father and she did love him. Meg said that Regina wanted to start visiting her father some when they got back. As for Lillian she is having a hard time with all the different feelings she is having to deal with but she has Oscar with her to help her understand them and heal. I saw them last week and it was a little sad, but with Oscar and his crazy life to mix with hers she will be ok in time if he doesn't drive her crazy first. My jaw and shoulder are healing nicely because we all know you can't keep a tough old bird down. As for Ronnie and I, we are almost back to normal and butting heads again, oh well, ain't love grand.

Lynda Hyde is a wife, mother and grandmother who enjoys reading and writing good mystery stories as well as quilting and other fun activities. She lives in a small town outside of Houston, Texas.

Coming Soon by Lynda Hyde

The Mystery of the Dead Dog Quilt

The Fat Quarter Mystery

The Longest Twelve Hours

Lynda Hyde

www.ingramcontent.com/pod-product-compliance
Lightning Source LLC
LaVergne TN
LVHW090958080826
845145LV00003B/1051

* 9 7 8 0 5 7 8 0 0 1 2 7 2 *